About the author

Born and raised in New Orleans, by day, a Bonsai enthusiast, by night a historian. I enjoy traveling to places with great history like my own. I have been surrounded by the history of this great city my whole life. After discovering family papers, I found my great-great grandfather's interview from 1913. It opened the door to history that is basically unknown, not only to New Orleans, but throughout the world. I hope you will enjoy these writings as much as I have researched every step he endured.

Survivor: 1851 Insurrection from New Orleans to Cuba

Dal Cousans

Survivor: 1851 Insurrection from
New Orleans to Cuba

TO: LARC
Enjoy THE History
— DAC

Dal Cousans

Vanguard Press

A CIP catalogue record for this title is
available from the British Library.

ISBN 978 1 784653 00 2

Vanguard Press is an imprint of
Pegasus Elliot MacKenzie Publishers Ltd.
www.pegasuspublishers.com

First Published in 2018

Vanguard Press
Sheraton House Castle Park
Cambridge England

Dedication

To my dad, Joseph "*Pat*" Cousans
and
My great-great grandfather,
William Cousans

Acknowledgments

Cindy Newton, who stayed by my side.

Chris Prevou, for your knowledge and support.

I NEVER GAVE UP...
Survivor: 1851 Insurrection from New Orleans to Cuba

CHAPTER 1
A NEW LIFE IN AMERICA

This is a true story, told by many generations of a brave and courageous man. The last known living survivor of the López Expedition of 1851, and that man is William Cousans. His last interview was in *The Times-Democrat* newspaper of New Orleans on Sunday, March 30, 1913 – he was eighty years old at the time. With a gleam in his eyes, he began to tell, with much detail, of that harrowing time in his life.

He witnessed so many things that one cannot but feel amazed at his story. It is a tale of intrigue, shock, amazement and, at last, freedom. Many generations came after these heroic men, who were lucky to survive such a calamitous event in their lives. William never gave up throughout the expedition and lived to tell his story.

William was a drugstore chemist in Biloxi, Mississippi, at the time of this interview. He was filling prescriptions with the skill and accuracy of a far younger man than his years, with many more to come. He was always telling stories of his life and the paper in New Orleans decided to interview him and print his story. Mrs. Julia Truitt Bishop sat quietly with William and every word intrigued her even more. He told her about the historic time of the men who suffered and survived after they joined as filibusters in the López insurrection.

It was a hundred and sixty-five years ago. The men, with their courage and valor, faced one of the hardest times in their lives head on, not foreseeing the outcome of this expedition. Most accounts of its deeds must be taken with a great deal of trust. Such things as López's attempt to seize Cuba from the Spanish stronghold are either wholly unknown to the people of New Orleans now, or so far in the past that the events are so vague it is as if one were to peer through the mists of time to perceive the events. New Orleans was filled with a diversity of people and, one day, it changed simply with the nationality in which you were born. The López Expedition turned man against man, with the hatred towards Spanish. Yet, William told his story as though it happened yesterday. A time in his life he would never forget.

The brave men who went with General López did not know what to expect. They were looking for adventure and ended up fighting for their lives instead of independence for the Cuban people. They faced unknown danger and hunger every day, hoping they would make it off the island alive.

Mr. William Cousans was born in Lincolnshire, England, on July 6, 1832. His parents, Matthew and Mary Ann Cousans, wanted so much more for their young son. They secured passage on a ship for the young William to cross the Atlantic Ocean to the United States. They were able to give William the funds to help begin his new life. He arrived in America in the spring of 1851, at the age of eighteen. He had the irresistible impulse in his blood to see the new world and was looking for excitement and adventure. He was enthusiastic to greet America head on and to make a prosperous life for himself. His first destination was Iowa, where he secured employment working as a clerk in one of the general stores.

William was very good with numbers and he settled into his position quickly. Day to day life in Iowa, however, was not much for him and he wanted to seek more challenges in his life. He managed to accumulate two hundred dollars by saving all the money he could. In today's time, that would be close to six thousand dollars. He wrote letters to his parents asking for advice on what he should do with his savings. His parents suggested he should invest the money so he could prosper and succeed in life. William settled down in Iowa but still felt like there was something missing in his life.

One day, a couple of gentleman walked into the store and told him stories of their trip to New Orleans. He was intrigued by the conversation and anxiously wanted to learn more. They spoke of New Orleans as the biggest city with the most important port in the south. The city was growing more every day with people from all over the world. They spoke of the rich and unique culture of the citizens and the architectural, French influenced, designs of the buildings. Some of the buildings had their own secluded courtyards. They described the decorative wrought iron balconies and the large arched doorways. William was fascinated by every word as he learned more about New Orleans. The land surrounding New Orleans was abound with the grandeur of the old oak trees with their branches hanging like hands as if to embrace the ground. The men continued their story with the legend of Jean Lafitte, the privateer who helped Andrew Jackson in the final Battle of New Orleans in 1812. William learned of the swamps surrounding New Orleans with their endless waterways, as Spanish moss hung from the gnarled cypress trees. The men spoke of magnificent plantations scattered along the banks of the Mississippi River, in all the elegance of the South. When the men left the store, William knew this was where he wanted to be, and little did he know that it would be in New Orleans that his life would change forever.

William gathered his belongings, acquired a passage on one of the paddleboats going to New Orleans, and began his journey down the Mississippi River. He met people of all statures and backgrounds on board – going for business, pleasure and to start a new life, like himself. It seemed that everyone on the boat was talking about the Vieux Carré, (French for Old Square – today it is known as the French Quarter). It was during this journey that he heard the story of General López and that he was looking for filibusters to join him on his next expedition to Cuba.

The men, who spoke of López to William, were excited on hearing the news of men gathering in New Orleans for Cuban Independence. William thought this was maybe the adventure he was finally seeking in his life and wanted to learn more. Anticipation followed him, along with others, as they traveled south getting closer to New Orleans. This was William's first trip down the mighty Mississippi River and he witnessed farms, small towns and grand plantations dotted about the banks. They made occasional stops along the way to pick up or drop off passengers. Standing by the railing, William saw farms with an abundance of livestock and knew this life would not interest him. He came from the refined living in England, but still he wanted more.

Arriving in New Orleans, William saw how the city was alive all the time. Nothing like the slower pace he had experienced in Iowa. When the paddleboat arrived at the dock, he noticed a streetcar being pulled by horses on the cobblestone streets. It was the first time he saw a streetcar. The streets were filled with people walking to and from their destinations. One of his first stops was the French Market along the banks of the Mississippi River. The French Market was a variety of people who would sell and buy their fruits, vegetables, pellets, livestock and anything else you could ever want.

He started walking down Decatur Street and was amazed at the balconies with their wrought iron designs. He walked until eventually he was standing in the square with the St. Louis Cathedral. He spoke with a gentleman on the corner and learned that it was called "Plaza de Armas". The gentleman said that following the 1812 battle of New Orleans, it was renamed Jackson Square for the victorious General Jackson. William listened as the man continued and learned more about the filibusters wanting to join the López expedition. The excitement seemed to be with every man wanting to join this campaign and the conversations grew more and more animated. William's two hundred dollars were gladly thrown in to be a part of this adventure. He followed with all the joy of youth but also naïve of what it meant to be a filibuster. Men waited anxiously hoping they would be chosen for the expedition with General López. Filibusters are irregular soldiers who act without authority from their own government, and are generally motivated by financial gain, or the thrill of adventure. William knew this was the adventure he was looking for.

It is a remarkable fact that this was not the first attempt General López had made to free Cuba from the Spaniards. About one year prior, he had led a similar expedition to Cuba, landing in the village of Cardenas, and had conquered it. This was called the Cardenas Expedition in 1850.

However, Cardenas was recaptured by the Spanish, and those filibusters barely escaped to Key West following López's departure. The stigma of that unsuccessful expedition surrounded him. However, being the leader that López was, he was to set out for Cuba again. The people responded with enthusiasm through the press that was printed and the stories taken from that voyage.

CHAPTER 2
NARCISO LÓPEZ

Narciso López was born in Carcas, Venezuela, on November 2, 1797. He began his military career by joining the Spanish Army in the attempt to suppress Simon Bolivar's movement. After Spain's withdrawal from Venezuela in 1823, he resided in Cuba and Spain where he received prestigious military and political posts. He was the Military Governor of Madrid, a Major-General in the Spanish army and a Senator in the Spanish Cortez for the province of Seville. López joined the fraternity in Spain and became a Freemason. He relied extensively on the international fraternity to accomplish his military plans and later belonged to Solomon's Lodge, No. 1, in Savannah. He accordingly resigned his high position, and went to Cuba in the company of his friend, Don Geronimo Valdes, who appointed him to be Assistant to the Captain-General of the central province of Cuba.

López married Maria Dolores, the sister of the Count of Pozos Dulces, a prominent United States educated Creole planter. He was Cuban by adoption and had great affection for his country. He had achieved the rank of General in the Spanish Army. López lost his post in Cuba when the governorship changed hands in 1843. On the removal of Valdes, López applied himself to the task he was preparing in his mind about freeing Cuba when he was no longer in office. After failing in a few business ventures, he became intrigued with the anti-Spanish movement in Cuba. In 1848, the Spanish started to arrest Cuban revolutionaries, and López decided to flee to the United States so he would not be captured.

He was a born leader and his demeanor and confidence stemmed from his experience with his military endeavors. López was a man of supremacy, courage, daring, and was physically endowed with great endurance. All of these qualities led men from as many as a dozen different states to rally for his cause to return to Cuba once again. His supporters filled a variety of roles. One example was that he could not speak English, or very little, and had followers act as translators during his planning of the expedition. He drew many sympathizers and interested parties to him, besides the young William.

López focused his recruiting on the southern United States. He made his headquarters in New Orleans and began his plans for his expedition. López was a slave trade supporter and knew the advantages for the South with an independent Cuba. Southern political and business owners were attracted to the idea to annex Cuba to ensure the continuation of slavery and trade with Cuba. This would offer the South political advantages. Success in Cuba would also open new markets to New Orleans merchants and lucrative investments to real estate speculators.

Men with significant influence came to him from the entire southern region. New Orleans had many Spanish citizens and businesses already established and were big supporters for Cuban independence. During that time, López received the warmest encouragement and welcome from the citizens of New Orleans. Every available man was ready to sign up for the expedition, as news spread throughout New Orleans. Southern Federal Officials felt sympathy for the Cuban cause and refused to stop the expedition.

Most of the men came from peaceful towns and cities, with no military training. They were sons of southern planters, clerks and even businessmen who wanted to sign up for the expedition. New Orleans businessmen joined the López committees and backed him for this endeavor because of declining economic fortunes.

In late January of 1851, López instructed Colonel Ambrosio José Gonzales, who had joined him in previous expeditions, to recruit men in Columbus, Atlanta, Macon and Savannah. He was told to gather supplies, ammunition and horses. Gonzales had been hidden by planters in coastal Georgia and South Carolina, awaiting more information from López regarding the upcoming expedition. They kept in contact by secret courier mail using special code names. In the spring, he obtained assistance from the Georgians, all that he could desire. Companies of volunteers and military men were formed in many parts of the State. Thousands of dollars were contributed and were sent to

Honorable John L. O'Sullivan in New York to purchase the steamer *Cleopatra* for transport. From the expedition the year before, the armament had been saved and was brought to the coast of Georgia. This secret cache of supplies was stored at the plantation of Mr. David Bailey. When the supplies were secured, Gonzales telegraphed López and then went to Jacksonville by railroad to await further instructions.

A Northerner, traveling in the South, heard of López and the filibusters' plot to invade Cuba. He disagreed with the plans of the invasion and reported the detailed intentions of the expedition to New York Senator Hamilton Fish, who immediately passed the news to President Millard Fillmore. After hearing the news of the expedition, President Fillmore seized the *Cleopatra* in New York, in late April to impede the arrival of the steamer to the filibusters in Jacksonville.

Excitement traveled throughout New Orleans and the surrounding towns about the expedition. López's main supporters came from the south as he predicted. The soldiers who did sign up were paid for their services. It was widely believed from the citizens that his main goal for the expedition was the annexation of Cuba to the United States. López did win the financial and political support of many Southerners including the editor of the New Orleans *Daily True Delta* newspaper, Laurence J. Sigur.

Laurence Sigur was one of the principal owners of the New Orleans *Daily True Delta* newspaper. He was an exiled Cuban patriot with extreme wealth. The New

Orleans *Daily True Delta* had a wide circulation, reaching towns and cities all over the South. It emphasized its influence towards building up an interest in Cuban independence. This would result in hopes of a strong expedition of filibusters and military men from the South going to Cuba. The prime reason why New Orleans newspapers published only favorable stories concerning the Cuban invasion of 1851, was the promise of sugar plantations in Cuba to the supporters.

General López lived in the home of Laurence Sigur and enjoyed his wealth, to his convenience. Sigur and López received the support of local merchants and business men by showing them the benefits that the New Orleans' economy would reap from the possession of Cuba.

One of the men who became quite interested in Cuba was Felix Huston. He was a Louisiana planter and an Eyes of States' Rights advocate. He realized that a victory in Cuba would be a strong step in forming an independent southern republic. He became the Chairman of the fund-raising activities, by the end of August 1851 in New Orleans, for the López Expedition.

Towards the last week in July, recruiting and organizing for the proposed expedition reached its height. A large amount of men from Cincinnati, were said to be en route to New Orleans to join the expedition. A Kentucky sympathizer for López enlisted men and was to pay them sixty to seventy dollars a month. From all over the South, hundreds of young adventures, including William, gathered in New Orleans to join the filibustering expedition. The men stayed hidden and traveled in small groups, using back roads to avoid being noticed by federal authorities. Since López was a Freemason, he received useful and beneficial backing from members of the Solomon's Lodge No. 20 in Jacksonville. No other filibustering expedition had as much support in New Orleans and from the South.

The rebel leaders in Cuba contacted López and other Cuban exiles living in the United States. They pleaded for his support and help in their fight for freedom. American news sources in Havana declared the island would be independent from Spain in sixty days. The Cubans knew that General López would be the man to help lead them with their cause.

CHAPTER 3
SUPPORTERS FOR THE EXPEDITION

New Orleans was faced with a recession in 1851 with the cotton market and official constraints. A decline in the mid-western trade and the loss of traditional cotton markets was the cause of aggressive urban competitors. New Orleans businessmen, with the aid of lawyers, journalists and politicians, took advantage of this and actively worked on behalf of López's plans for entering Cuba. The open conduct of business from the fact that bonds were floated in which a considerable sum of money was raised for the main purpose of the expedition. General López sold these Cuban bonds at ten per cent of their face value. By printing and selling these bonds, López was able to raise fifty thousand dollars. The purchase of such bonds could dramatically transform an investor's economic status in New Orleans. The chance to increase their income was more enticing for an adventure like this and most businessmen were eager to help López. Many business leaders who supported the López expedition had hopes of reviving the city's economy. The severe 1851 reduction in tobacco and grain prices increased the curiosity of nine grocers and two tobacco merchants to raise money to support the expedition. Limited job opportunities and economic decline in New Orleans were the primary reasons why many lawyers, journalists, and merchants participated in the events to help raise money.

Three thousand, one hundred and seventy-seven seagoing vessels docked in New Orleans on the banks of the Mississippi River between 1847 and 1848. This number dropped in 1850 and 1851 to two thousand and nineteen. This was thirty-six percent less than two years prior. New Orleans had the highest levee taxes in the United States and captains of ocean-traveling ships and river steamboats complained about the taxes and fees that they were required to pay for docking their craft. Every vessel that arrived in the New Orleans port was subjected to paying a five dollar fee to the port warden and an additional amount to the harbor master.

General López first offered the command of the expedition to Jefferson Davis, who had distinguished himself in the Battle of Buena Vista during the Mexican American War in 1847. Mr. Davis was a United States senator of Mississippi at the time when he was approached by López. He met with the senator, offering him one hundred thousand dollars and a coffee plantation in Cuba if he chose to accept. Jefferson seriously considered his offer, but, to the relief of his wife, he declined his proposal. López knew that having a man of his distinguished military qualities would only benefit his expedition because of his leadership. After Senator Davis declined, he then recommended his good friend from the Mexican American War, Major Robert E. Lee. Lee considered his same offer and pondered over the thought, but turned him down as well.

Unfortunately, not everyone accepted López's views on planning a filibustering expedition from the United States to liberate Cuba. There was a tremendous amount of risk involved with the United States government, and Davis and Lee recognized these problems while making their decisions. It is safe to say that, if Jefferson Davis or Robert E. Lee had agreed to command this expedition, the outcome could have been considerably different, not only for Cuba but for the United States. As history dictates, Jefferson Davis and Robert E. Lee were both destined to play a major part in the American Civil War. Colonel William Crittenden was living in New Orleans and was an officer at the Custom House, located in New Orleans. The Custom House was also known as the main post office and federal court and was located on the corner of Canal Street and North Peters Street. He graduated from the military academy at West Point, and fought in the Mexican American War. Crittenden resigned his commission in the regular Army of the United States for the sole purpose of joining López in the expedition to set Cuba free from Spain. This was quite an accomplishment for a man of twenty-eight years old. López picked a valuable leader in his cause with Colonel Crittenden, who was so highly connected in the United States, socially, politically and officially. His uncle was John J. Crittenden, Attorney General of the United States. Having this influence was beneficial to López and his expedition who took full advantage of Crittenden.

Colonel Crittenden attracted volunteers to the López Expedition in Southern and Mid-western towns. He promised the young recruits Cuban sugar plantations of their own and enticing cash bonuses for their enlistment. Crittenden knew the appeal of his offers were also enticing to the numerous young clerks and farm hands who were already discouraged with their present work situations – the clerks worked long and heavy work schedules and were not paid very well. William was one of these clerks and found no excitement from the day to day struggles of being a clerk at the time. Crittenden's speeches also intrigued many sons of Southern planters who faced the increasingly difficult task of obtaining farms. The inflation rapidly increased the price of land and slaves to prospective buyers in the area. The hopes of a possible sugar plantation of their own made them eagerly join the cause with López.

As early as July 23rd, the press was filled with the news in New Orleans of the revolution in Cuba. While in progress, it was said: "The news is received with signs of general joy for everybody desires the emancipation of the beautiful little island."

On August 1st, one of the New Orleans papers said:

"It will be impossible, as it would be unnatural, to repress American's feelings of great joy at the spirit which is exhibiting itself in Cuba, of rejoicing at the success of the patriots, and of [the] zeal to join with them in the struggle and aid them to achieve independence. The fullness of the national heart will speak out and, while men will submit to the injunction of laws which forbid them from interfering in foreign quarrels in such a manner as to violate international compacts that are binding in our government, they will, without doubt, in thousands, think themselves justified in resuming the natural right of expatriation, which every man enjoys who will encounter the perils, and each one, with his life in his hand, go to succor the oppressed in Cuba in the struggle for liberty, as their fathers were succored by the chivalry of Europe."

The filibusters had several meeting places in New Orleans before they were to set sail for Cuba. One of the meetings took place in the old arcade, under the St. James Hotel. Here is where all the plans for the López Expedition were made. The local merchants and tradesmen conducted business in this building for meetings to support the neighborhoods above Canal Street. The coffee import meeting place in the arcade provided hundreds of social coffee roasters around the United States at a time when communication with coffee-producing countries and customers were slow and unreliable.

Since the filibusters worked in secrecy, confidential couriers were used, having code names throughout the South. They kept few records of their activities and meetings, destroying notes and documents, as they were ordered to do, as soon as decisions were made by the leaders of the expedition. This was because correspondence could be used as evidence of violation of the Neutrality Law of 1818. This law defines filibustering as a private endeavor by individuals to organize their own military expeditions to invade a country that is at peace with the United States. The Neutrality Act of 1818 specifically and strictly forbad such private military expeditions to take place. López continued his plans, even though he was fully aware of this law.

In July of 1851, López gave the word to his unorganized recruits to assemble quietly in New Orleans. Companies and regiments were gathered together in secrecy. William considered himself lucky as one of the chosen men who would take on this task. Laurence Sigur, the editor of the New Orleans *True Daily Delta* newspaper, was known to be the moving force behind the assembly of these men. He told the members of the expedition that, "A revolt was organized amongst the Creoles throughout Cuba." But everyone did not hold their tongue in these meetings as word spread quickly throughout New Orleans. Creoles are native-born persons of mixed European and African ancestry who can speak either French or Spanish.

Never in the history of New Orleans were people so advised and encouraged in a filibustering expedition. The people responded in a kind manner, as was evident in the press and from the story told by William.

The steamer *Pampero* arrived in New Orleans on Tuesday, July 29th, stating she had mechanical problems with the ship. Sigur purchased the *Pampero*, after he sold his ownership of the *True Daily Delta* newspaper for forty thousand dollars, to transport the filibusters in the expedition. López got excited, seeing the steamer for the first time, and started preparing the men to load the supplies for the campaign.

General López received valuable information from Colonel Crittenden through his position at the Customs House. The information he received was the *Pampero* was to be seized on Monday morning, August 4th, by government agents. After hearing this news, López gave explicit orders to Crittenden for the expedition to leave immediately on Sunday night instead of Monday as they had planned.

CHAPTER 4
THE EXPEDITION DEPARTS

Early morning on Sunday, August 3rd, a large crowd was gathered at what was known then as "The Bull's Head" at Lafayette Street Landing near Felicity Road by the Mississippi River. Yet still there were many supplies to be gathered, including coal needed for the voyage. This had delayed the *Pampero* till almost four o'clock that morning. López gave the order to Captain Armstrong Irvin Lewis to push full steam ahead and was assured the *Pampero* would have enough coal for sixteen days of sailing, according to his requirement for the expedition. Captain Lewis also steered the *Creole* in the previous Cardenas Expedition that ended successfully for a short period of time. He has been quoted in saying, "The *Pampero* is quite fast, and will run ahead of any of the war steamers." The crowd consisted of ten to twelve thousand as they cheered loudly for the filibusters.

Washington authorities tried to prevent the expedition from sailing, but the *Pampero* was able to cast off her lines from the dock. She started on her long voyage to their first stop at Key West.

The *Pampero* was the only ship which left New Orleans in that expedition, with four hundred and seventy-five men aboard. There were to be four or five boats. It still lies a mystery as to why only one ship left the dock that morning for Cuba when so many men were eargerly lined up at the Mississippi River. The great majority of the two thousand men remained at the dock, waiting for their opportunity to get out, but there was none. If there was a possibility of another ship carrying more filibusters, López's forces could have been much stronger when they reached Cuba.

Before departing, J. A. Kelly, an officer López had chosen to accompany him on the expedition, thanked merchants and businessmen for raising funds and supplies on behalf of the campaign. One of the journalists wrote an article in a paper of the day said, "Our New Orleans merchants have poured in, in their abundance, to the cause, and vessels are fully equipped and ready for sea with all the sinews and munitions of war." The staff aboard the *Pampero* were engineers who were Cubans and Hungarians along with a few Germans. The staff also had surgeons who were able to help with casualties of American troops and offer assistance to Spanish casualties as well.

The mighty Mississippi River has many twists and turns with strong currents that made the voyage slow. Other ships traveling on the river made it difficult for the *Pampero* to navigate the waters. The *Pampero*'s engines were not working properly at the time and she had to be towed towards the mouth of the river. Captain Lewis reported that, "His boilers were burnt out," from a collapsed fifteen-inch exhaust pipe. The malfunctions slowed the *Pampero* to a speed of eight knots instead of the usual fifteen. López insisted on leaving immediately and a temporary replacement pipe was installed while she was being towed. After about twelve miles below New Orleans, the *Pampero* stopped to take on board the German and Cuban Companies. These men were sent down previously the day before, where they were ordered to wait until the arrival of the *Pampero*.

Fifty or sixty miles heading south down the Mississippi River, the *Pampero* dropped anchor at Balize, Louisiana, to continue the work that needed to be done on the engines. This gave the officers ample time to organize the men and supplies on board.

The surgeons on board performed a physical examination of the men to see if they could make this long journey. Some of the men, about twenty-five, were sent back, as they were not going to withstand the hardships which they could meet in this expedition or felt they were too young for the voyage ahead. López wanted to reduce the over-crowded *Pampero* and released these men to be returned on the tender *Ben Adams* back to New Orleans.

Every foot of space on the *Pampero* was occupied by the unorganized men. Strewn about were knapsacks for the men, barrels, boxes with supplies, trunks and bags. These were strewn everywhere throughout the deck, including the men. The men were cramped together and had little walking room, but kept high hopes in their new adventure. Once the men had settled down, they were divided into nine companies and three regiments. These different companies were given certain sections on the ship and the staff restricted these men to their allotted space. The officers, however, had the luxury of having cabins below deck while the men stayed on the upper deck.

The *Pampero* remained anchored until the afternoon of Wednesday, August 6th. After getting her engines working properly, she left at about five o'clock that afternoon. When the *Pampero* reached the head of the passes leading towards the Gulf of Mexico, Captain Lewis received information from another pilot that a revenue cutter was waiting for them to arrive. A revenue cutter is an armed custom enforcement service ship. Learning the news of this cutter, they went down the northeast pass and were chased by the cutter but escaped from their sight. The cutter moved up to the head of the passes, blocking the river and made it impossible for any other boats to get out. The *Pampero* reached the mouth of the river which ends at the Gulf of Mexico and was then in open waters on her way to Key West. The night was clear and full of stars to help Captain Lewis navigate on the calm waters of the gulf. This provided perfect sailing conditions for the *Pampero*.

With all the men securely on board, an assessment was made of the muskets and supplies. They were unpacked and distributed to the men on August 7th. Every man had the task of cleaning the muskets they were assigned.

After hearing of the departure of the expedition from New Orleans on August 3rd, the government decided to take immediate steps. President Millard Fillmore sent warships to prevent the sailing of any reinforcements. The President sent the *Albany* and *Vixen* to sail along the coast of Cuba near Havana. The *Preble* and the *Dolphin* were sent to patrol other coasts along Cuba to observe other points of possible landing locations from the expedition. The President reiterated his earlier orders to the warships, warning any federal officials not to become associated with the filibusters by allowing any illegal activity to take place.

On Sunday, August 19th, the *Pampero* reached Key West, anchoring some distance from the shore possibly because of the violation of the Neutrality Law. After nearly five days at sea, the men were happy to see land again. The filibusters waited on board and had time to relax as they waited anxiously for instructions from General López.

Captain Lewis reported to López there was only enough coal for three more days. The miscalculation of the amount of coal when being loaded in New Orleans was due to the hasty departure of the *Pampero* leaving the dock. The machinery that was replaced on the *Pampero* could have been a factor in her ability to push fifteen knots as predicted. She was known as one of the fastest steamers out of New Orleans.

Information soon arrived for López in the form of a letter waiting for him at Key West from a well-known informant of his in Havana, who would guide him for landing. He had confidence in this person with news from Cuba and trusted him. He read the letter, stating, "Pinar del Rio, and almost all of the Vuelta de Abijo, were in open insurrection, and that he better proceed thither at once with his force."

The *Pampero* pulled up anchor and left Key West at approximately ten o'clock in the evening and was at sea with ninety miles ahead of her. After receiving the letter at Key West, López decided not to go with his original plans of landing at Puerto Principe. He wanted to go to St. John's River in Jacksonville, Florida to pick up more filibusters who were to meet him there and gather more provisions. López called a meeting with his officers on board to convey the contents of the letter. The officers all agreed that it was in their best interest to proceed at once to Vuelta de Abajor. The officers informed the filibusters of the landing at Bahia Honda by morning. As the men prepared their supplies, anticipation and excitement flowed throughout the ship.

During the night, the machinery was deemed not to be working properly and a decision was made to stop the *Pampero*'s engines for several hours. The *Pampero* floated with the strong currents of the gulf waters and drifted an unexpected distance eastward. Captain Lewis looked at the compass of the ship and informed López, he was receiving wrong readings because of the proximity and the amount of iron in the musket barrels.

The engines were repaired and the *Pampero* left at ten o'clock in the morning and was heading straight for the narrow entrance of Havana Harbor, instead of being off the coast of Bahia Honda. The filibusters found themselves in plain view of Morro Castle. Captain Lewis quickly steered the *Pampero* in a northwesterly direction to avoid being seen by the soldiers that were on the wall of the castle and men working on the shore. The filibusters hurriedly went below deck as ammunition was passed out in case of battle. They were prepared for an anticipated attack from the Spanish. López watched closely through his spyglass at the narrow passage between the Morro and Punta Fort, no more than a quarter mile in width and expected to see one of the Spanish war steamers following his getaway.

Unfortunately, they were seen from the Morro and the Spanish vessel *Pizarro,* while patrolling in Havana Harbor, was sent out to investigate the suspicious ship. The *Pizarro* was slow getting out and did not come within sight of the *Pampero* that day. The *Pampero* quickly got away at full steam ahead of the *Pizarro.*

With the *Pizarro* behind them, López was now looking for any Spanish schooner from which he wanted to take a pilot to help with his directions. Captain Lewis was not familiar with the Cuban coast and help was certainly needed now. The wind was calm as López noticed a schooner in the distance and the *Pampero* was able to catch up with her at about three o'clock in the afternoon. The Spanish schooner was named the *Cecilia.* The *Cecilia* raised their Spanish red and yellow flag, but soon saw the large amount of men on board the *Pampero* and slowed down. They knew they didn't have a chance to outrun the *Pampero.* The captain of the *Cecilia* recognized the men as being part of the expedition that everyone proclaimed would be arriving in Cuba. They lowered their flag quicker than they raised it. The *Pampero* pulled up at the side of the *Cecilia* and López's men went aboard and seized the captain of the ship. López ordered the captain, Don Felipe Torre, and a mate, D. Luis Diaz, of the schooner, to board the *Pampero* at once. Although reluctant, Captain Torre obeyed López's command. He stood before López, and demanded any news of the landing of the filibusters. The captain replied by saying that he had not heard anything of such an expedition. He probably said that to save his own life and the lives of his crew. He was told to remain on board the *Pampero* and act as pilot to navigate the shores. López looked directly at him and made it understood that he would be shot if he tried to escape or deceive him in any way. The captain listened to every word López said to him. He began to cry and weep as he knew the position López had put him in. Such a service – helping with the expedition – would result in death by his own government. After the captain gave directions, López then released the captain and ordered him to steer his schooner towards a different place other than the direction of the *Pampero*. López had hoped this would prevent the captain from coming into contact with other Spanish vessels and divulge any information of their whereabouts. Soon the *Cecilia* was no longer to be seen from the *Pampero* again.

Consequently, the *Pampero* was headed straight for Bahia Honda. The devoted filibusters, who started so anxiously from New Orleans, were going into a trap through the arrival of the letter that López received in Key West. The trap was set for López and his troops by the Spanish Captain-General de la Concha. The Spanish

General Enna, second-in-command, led seven hundred soldiers on the *Pizarro* from Havana, when Spanish intelligence discovered López's intentions of entering Cuba. This was the ultimate Spanish trick. General López did not know what he was about to face during his expedition with the filibusters.

CHAPTER 5
LANDING IN CUBA

The men on board the *Pampero* were preparing for landing. They were issued blue shirts and gray pants – the uniform assigned to each man for the expedition. The equipment given to each man were a knapsack, a pouch for cartridges, a slung flask for water and a blanket. They were also given a musket and a bayonet with eighty to one hundred cartridges.

With nightfall quickly approaching, the pilot was unsure of the depth of the waters to the entrance of Bahia Honda. López studied the land and sent a small boat to the shore for reconnaissance. As they approached the shore, the men encountered a few Spanish soldiers ready for gunfire. Discovering the soldiers, they silently returned, unnoticed, back to the *Pampero* and relayed the events to General López about what had just occurred. They saw lights from lit torches on the shore; however, it was too dark for the men on board the *Pampero* to be seen from land. They escaped the sights of the Spanish. López thought that landing at Morrillo would be out of the Spanish eyes and safe for his men to land.

Around ten o'clock in the evening, the *Pampero* approached the coast, reaching closer to Morrillo – about sixty miles from Havana and approximately twelve miles west of Bahia Honda. The Spanish captain, whom they captured from the *Cecilia*, discovered the *Pampero* had grounded in the waters after missing the channel approaching Morrillo. He feared the load on the ship was too heavy for the shallow waters. They were only a mile from the shore. Captain Lewis knew this, once the supplies and men were removed, she would float again in high tide. The hour had come for the filibusters to leave the ship and begin their expedition. Before they were to leave, López spoke with his officers, saying the opportunity of withdrawing from the expedition was still open to the men. The officers announced to the men, that if there was any one who was not fully satisfied with the expedition thus far, they should return on the *Pampero* back to the United States. Not a single brave man spoke a word, nor moved from his position on the ship. Only two of the filibusters decided to return to the United States and it was because they fell sick on the voyage. They stood together, as one, to face the outcome and stand behind their General.

At approximately eleven o'clock, on the August 11th, the landing for the shores commenced at Morrillo. In the first boat was the Hungarian, General John Pragay, the Chief of Staff and second-in-command to reach the land. William remembers a few moving lights were visible on the shoreline as he watched silently from the *Pampero*. Shots were then heard and the men were not sure what happened. The boat returned with news of three or four men on land, who had fired at them when they approached the shore. The Creoles, to their surprise, aimed with the most hostile and deadly intentions. The men returned a few random shots at the Creoles when they turned and ran off into the darkness.

The moonlight shone brightly on the water and López's men could reach the shoreline without difficulty. A couple of fishing boats were found along the shore that helped the men and supplies land as fast as possible. The Creoles on shore kept the Spanish troops aware of any movements by the filibusters since landing at Morrillo.

With the men and supplies off the ship, Captain Lewis was hopeful that the *Pampero* would float again but, with the tide still not in, all they could do was wait. At around four o'clock in the morning, on August 12th, General López finally put his foot back on Cuban soil, along with his men and officers. He wore pantaloons and a white jacket, buttoned all the way up his neck, with a white collar embroidered with a single star. A red sash, fastened around his waist and over his shoulder, slung a spyglass in a leather case. The General was carrying no arms as he touched the soil. His sword and pistols were still with his baggage. The first thing López did was kneel and kiss the soil of his beloved Cuba.

Morrillo was a small village with only four houses, so there must have been a few inhabitants. The first thing everyone noticed was the buildings were open, empty and completely deserted. The shore seemed completely without inhabitants, they had deserted before they landed. The doors and windows were left open as if the people eagerly left their homes. They were expecting horses, carts and additional supplies as they had been informed, and led to believe, but none were found.

After all the supplies were unloaded, the men were finally relieved to reach Cuba. They were ordered to rest and await instructions from the officers. Guards were posted to keep a watchful eye for the Spanish. Unfortunately, the men had their first attack, which were mosquitos. They swarmed by the thousands on the shore as the men covered their faces with a handkerchief and gloves to protect themselves. They also encountered land crabs running about everywhere – so resting was simply optional at this point.

The high tide returned and the *Pampero* could sail on the high waters of the gulf. The *Pampero* was instructed by López to carry home the news of their landing in Cuba with the letters the men wrote to loved ones of their journey. As the men rested, they looked out towards the water and had the simple joy of seeing the *Pampero* floating once again. At nine o'clock in the morning, as the men were preparing to march for Las Pozas, they knew there was no turning back as they saw the *Pampero* leave.

The *Pampero* steamed towards Jacksonville, Florida, to the St. Johns River, under orders from General López. Letters were sent to his friends instructing them of the change in course and to proceed immediately to the Central Department of the island. López hoped that the *Pampero* would bring back more filibusters along with howitzers, field pieces, rifles and more cartridges from Jacksonville. As the steamer approached Jacksonville, however, Captain Lewis learned of American naval vessels near Jacksonville, where it was watched with interest by officials of the government administration. This discouraging news prevented Captain Lewis from sailing the *Pampero* to the city. The *Pampero* headed back towards New Orleans where another large force of filibusters were anxiously waiting for the arrival, just like in Jacksonville.

"After the men and ammunition had been landed," said William, "the *Pampero* got away, though it was chased by a Spanish man-of-war. Here, the forces were divided."

The filibusters gathered the supplies and carried all they could as López was anxious to quickly move his men. General Pragay stopped General López and persuaded him to detach Colonel Crittenden and his men to stay and guard the ammunition and supplies until carts could be found and they could return later.

The men were told that if they were caught stealing, or guilty of any such act, they would be severely punished. López started the march with his men to the small village of Las Pozas, approximately ten miles inland.

López left Crittenden, with over one hundred of the best men from the expedition, to establish a base camp. Crittenden then divided his battalion into three separate companies, under the commands of Captain J. A. Kelly, Captain James Saunders and Captain Victor Kerr.

Crittenden took an inventory of the supplies, which consisted of one hundred and fifty muskets, two barrels of cartridges and four barrels of powder. Among the other supplies was the officer's baggage and the flag of the expedition. General López's personal papers and printed proclamations were sealed in his valise. Crittenden would now wait for the carts to arrive from López.

CHAPTER 6
BATTLE AT LAS POZAS

A large force of insurgents was to be expected by López and his men when they reached Las Pozas. As the men marched, they suffered intensely from the heat and mosquitos. The swarm of mosquitos lasted for the first two or three miles into their march inland. The men had extensive bites and whelps, but they continued forward and followed López. They traveled a short distance when they came upon four horses that were healthy and in good condition for riding. They had saddles for mounting, as if someone just left them there. The officers used the horses quickly to their advantage while the men continued on foot

The filibusters reached Las Pozas around two o'clock that afternoon. They marched up the small hill till they reached the top of the ridge. This was the highest point of the village and also the entrance. The village was surrounded by hills with a forest on one side and a large corn field on the other. They had about fifty houses along the road and would slightly descend once going through to the other side.

General López later learned that most of the inhabitants of the little village were ordered by the Spanish authorities to leave at once before the filibusters arrived. They did find owners of two stores and a few men still in their homes. William also remembered – he was wondering why there were so few people in the village just as he noticed on the shoreline when they first landed.

Once arriving at Las Pozas, López immediately ordered men to locate carts to send them back to Crittenden for the supplies. An hour and a half later, eight men accompanied the carts to go to Crittenden and have him join López as fast as possible before daybreak. Having the men travel at night would be the best thing to escape the intense heat during the day and to avoid the Spanish.

Shortly after the men left with the carts for Crittenden at Morrillo, a local Creole arrived in Las Pozas from Bahia Honda. He informed López that the Spanish had found out about the arrival of his troops landing on shore. The Spanish frigate *Esperanza*, who had pursued them earlier, informed Havana of their arrival. The Spanish troops had previously arrived in Bahia Honda and were awaiting more orders from their Captain General to advance forward. López knew he needed time to train and drill his men, who were not ready to battle the Spanish. The more experienced men with military training stayed back with Crittenden. Guards were quickly posted at different points of the village and kept a watchful eye for any intrusion.

As soon as López received the news about the Spanish troops, he immediately sent direct orders to Crittenden. This order was told to Major Louis

Schlesinger in Spanish from General López. The order was then translated into English on paper, written by Major Louis Schlesinger. The order was then handed back to López who in turn gave the message to the Creole who informed him of the Spanish troops whom he felt could be trusted. Crittenden was ordered to leave the heavy baggage and supplies and proceed at once to join him that evening.

The Creole ran swiftly and passed the oxen pulling the carts. He reached Crittenden about an hour and a half before the carts had arrived. The letter ordered him to march forward and abandon the supplies and join him expeditiously. Crittenden received the order from López and gathered his men to move forward. López's men settled down for the evening, with the tropical breeze, and remained in good spirits. The harassment of mosquitos and croaking frogs were their only company that night.

The sun rose the next morning, August 13th and General López still did not see or hear back from Crittenden. He was worried that the orders he sent, and the carts, must have been cut off in some way by the Spanish although there was no way to be sure. López knew that Crittenden and his troops were a strong force required for the success of his expedition and this weighed heavily on his thoughts throughout that morning. The men awoke and were immediately ordered to commence drilling and exercises. In the meantime, a few men had killed some cattle to provide food for the men so they could have a decent breakfast.

Around eight o'clock in the morning, the men heard muskets being fired from one of the houses near the village's entrance. The filibusters said, "The enemy, the enemy," and the men reached for their weapons to return the fire. The house was occupied by the advanced Spanish guards who stayed hidden until the right moment to attack the filibusters.

López later learned the men were not at their posts and were having breakfast with the other filibusters. This left the filibusters wide open for an attack from the Spanish. The Spanish troops arrived and positioned themselves on a high hill just on the side of the village. López ordered the Cuban company at once to charge the house, with their bayonets raised and ready, to remove the Spanish guards. López unaware of the Spanish troops, had taken their position and begun to fire at them. The filibusters had a strong advantage and took cover under the trees and slopes of the hill to gain a better shot. They fired at the Spanish and the sound of blasts surrounded William and the other men. The battle lasted about three-quarters of an hour. The Spanish soldiers slowly disappeared into the hills and they were last seen going into the valley.

When López and his men first reached Las Pozas, he had nearly three hundred men, while the Spanish that attacked them that morning were over eight hundred. Thirty-five filibusters were killed or wounded badly and the Spanish had one hundred and eighty dead, not including their wounded.

Their bloody bodies were scattered throughout the

ridge and within the village. The wounded Spanish, found in the hills, were then brought back to the village. The men tried to take care of the wounded Spanish as best they could. The filibusters went out and gathered ammunition and supplies from the dead Spanish soldiers, as this would be greatly needed.

General López was on horseback and escaped the fire during the battle. He believed he was not injured due to the poor aim of the Spanish soldiers, aiming too high. He rode throughout the village to check on the condition of his men and for any wounded. With a lit cigar in his mouth, he patted them on their backs, yelling, "Bravo, bravo, Americano!" This was the little English he spoke and it encouraged the men to continue with the expedition.

Major Schlesinger, under López at Las Pozas, recruited five volunteers to encounter the risk of going to Crittenden to inform him of the victory the men had just accomplished. They were told to give him another route to avoid the Spanish troops. General López gave Major Schlesinger explicit orders again, in General López's name, to inform Crittenden to join them at Las Pozas before twelve that evening. The volunteers traveled back on the same road they marched on to Las Pozas and were told to stay to the left side of the main road to avoid being seen by the Spanish. That side of the road had many trees to hide behind. in case they were to encounter the enemy. If they heard any noise, or spotted the enemy, they were to send back one man, as soon as they could, with the note, so it would not fall into Spanish hands.

The volunteers returned unharmed to the village about nine o'clock. They reported to López that they encountered too many Spanish soldiers along the road while trying to reach Crittenden. They also said they had not seen or heard anything concerning the whereabouts of Crittenden and his men. López spoke with his officers and decided to send a Creole they found hiding in the village with a similar order written for Crittenden. López was increasingly agitated and told the Creole that he would give him one hundred dollars on his return or otherwise he would burn his house to the ground. The man agreed, but still López was not sure he could be trusted and might go straight to the Spanish troops. López predicted there would be more Spanish troops coming and he wanted to prepare Crittenden to attack the enemy from the rear and the flank.

CHAPTER 7
UNTIMELY CONCERNS

After Crittenden received the carts, he realized the oxen that were sent would not be enough to pull the overloaded carts filled with the supplies. He made the decision to send back one of the drivers, ahead of the others, for more oxen. Crittenden started for López at eleven o'clock in the evening from Morrillo. He took his company and slowly marched for Las Pozas, some ten miles ahead. They traveled at the rate of about one mile an hour, and after every hundred yards the oxen would stop, refusing to draw. The oxen continued to struggle to pull the carts, with great difficulty, on the roads that were filled with rocks and holes. The soldiers expended a great many profanities and useless blows from the butts of their muskets on the backs of the weary animals. They started removing large quantities of dead weight such as carpet bags and trunks belonging to the officers, from the carts, to relieve the weight for the oxen.

Nearly five miles into the slow march, the troops stopped at the local country store. They were now half way between Morrillo and Las Pozas. As the men were resting and eating, they were surprisingly attacked by a large number of Spanish troops. Although the Spanish were repelled, Crittenden was unable to start his march for Las Pozas in time before the Spanish troops returned the attack again. Pushing back the aggressive Spanish troops, Crittenden took eighty of his men and charged after them. Captain Kelly was ordered to remain in his position to guard the supplies until Crittenden returned.

Finally, at about ten thirty in the morning, López spoke with two filibusters who entered the village with a Creole guide. They informed him that Captain Kelly and his company of forty men, part of Crittenden's company, were hiding in the woods just a few miles away. Captain Kelly was unsure of who actually occupied the village of Las Pozas, whether it was the Spanish or López's troops. Crittenden was hesitant on the order he received from López, to proceed without the supplies. This decision caused a delay of Crittenden and his men joining López earlier and possibly, not obeying the written orders that were previously sent to him.

Captain Kelly, and the assigned men under him, were guided by the Creole driver of the carts that carried the supplies. He led them through the thick bushes and woods where they stayed hidden until the guide could go to the village. When the guide reached Las Pozas, he saw that López and his men were still there. He reported back to Captain Kelly, that Las Pozas was indeed occupied by López and the filibusters.

López ordered Major Schlesinger to return with the guide that came in earlier with the two men – to go back to Captain Kelly's position where he and his men were hiding and bring them to Las Pozas. López was eager to get the filibusters ready for the march to the mountains.

At about two o'clock in the morning on the 14th, López ordered the men to break camp at Las Pozas and to move forward with their march. The men had mixed emotions from the battle they had endured at Las Pozas, as they began under the clear night sky. William started to wonder what was going to happen next. They continued on a small footpath which crossed a small creek at the rear of the village, heading towards the mountains. López heard from some Creoles, about six miles away, the local military and civil authorities were waiting for them. He hoped to surprise and capture them to learn more information as to the whereabouts of the Spanish troops.

A few of the men, who received wounds from the battle at Las Pozas, could not walk on their own. Carrying these men would make it difficult for their escape to the mountains. These unfortunate men left behind were dying and eventually killed by the advanced guards of the Spanish, who were tracking the filibusters. The Spanish troops took no mercy on these men – they saw them as the enemy. They were never seen again.

The men were getting tired from the extra weight they had accumulated from the Spanish soldiers, as they continued in single file. They came upon a farm house around nine o'clock on the same morning and were in much need of rest. The men unloaded their packs and, due to the graciousness of the owner of the house, enjoyed a meal of oxen, plantains and corn. López thought the owner of the farm house was doing this for the future Republic of Cuba. More likely so he would not be shot.

After the men finished their meal and rested, they resumed their march around three o'clock that afternoon. López did not have the maps he was supposed to receive from Crittenden when he was to meet up with him. The maps were important, containing topographical areas of the Cuban region. These maps were very useful for military operations. However, he did possess a pocket compass and was able to find Creole guides available at different points along the way. The Creoles were not exactly content to be in the company of the filibusters, knowing they could be shot at any moment from either their government or the filibusters. As the sun began to go down, the men arrived at a small farm house near a little creek. They were ready to rest again after a long march. The officers gave the orders to prepare the camp and they would be there overnight. Guards were posted at various points in case of an attack.

In the meantime, Crittenden stayed together with the remaining two companies. They had been separated from Major Kelly since the thirteenth. The men kept a watchful eye in case the Spanish should return. Crittenden decided to take another road to reach López. But they were greeted head on by the remaining Spanish force that had fought with López earlier. Crittenden's men retreated into the thick bushes and stayed hidden from the enemy. Crittenden spoke with his officers who had remained with him and due to the heavy loss and casualties of his men, decided to head back for the seashore. Crittenden's men had not eaten in the past two days and were near starvation and weak from fighting the Spaniards. Hot temperatures soared as the sun rose high in the sky. Some of the men who received wounds were helped by the other men who were still able to make the journey. He decided the force, now being too small to reach López, could do nothing more to help with the expedition and decided to leave. Crittenden took the surviving men and headed for the coast where they first landed. They waited for nightfall so that their chances of being seen would be less than during the day. When they reached the shoreline that night, they found four fishing boats that were left abandon.

Most of the men boarded these boats, while the others continued walking on through the village. They quickly boarded and headed northwest towards New Orleans. They were hoping to be seen by an American vessel or American power, since they had no means of defense of their own.

As the men huddled in the small boats, dehydration and fatigue was taking a toll on them. The waves rushed and pushed against the boats as they floated out to sea. The men hoped that freedom was within their grasp and finally away from the island. Being destitute and starving, the men could not take it anymore and returned at daybreak to the shoreline to find food and water.

Several days passed before López received the news that Crittenden returned to the shoreline where they had first landed. Crittenden attempted to leave the island with about fifty men and López's fears were confirmed.

CHAPTER 8
CRITTENDEN'S CAPTURE

The Spanish steamer *Habanero* left Bahia Honda, searching the shoreline for any of López's troops or camps. They stayed along the shoreline by Playtas and Morrillo in hopes they would find more expeditions that were to be seen. The Spanish spoke with a few people in the village around seven o'clock in the morning in Morrillo, and were informed that most of the men escaped the night before, around ten o'clock, in four fishing boats. The Spanish quickly returned onto the steamers in search of the fishing boats.

The *Habanero* searched for hours and could not locate any of the boats that left with Crittenden and his men. The Spanish believed that Crittenden's men followed the rocks along the shoreline. The *Habanero* pushed further along the coast and saw one of the boats and were able to capture the men. They located the second and third boats upon the rocks near the shore. A couple of small boats were then lowered from the *Habanero,* with the officers and troops, to continue their pursuit of the filibusters. The filibusters reached the rocks to make their escape from the Spanish. The Spanish troops were quickly behind and closing the distance between them. Two of the filibusters managed to escape, but the Spanish decided not to chase after them since they were unarmed. The Spanish located the fourth boat near the rocks at Cayo Levisa, approximately ninety miles west of Havana. Crittenden's fate with the expedition ended when the Spanish captured him on the afternoon of August 15th.

Crittenden and his men were captured by Admiral Bustillos of the steamer *Habanero,* and were deemed as prisoners of the Spanish. They arrived on August 16th, at one thirty in the morning, in Havana. They were chained together like captured animals for many hours. The chains rubbed on their wrist and ankles causing their skin to blister and bleed. Their hands were swollen to double their normal size. They were unaware of what would happen to them next. The men were then transferred, at three o'clock the same morning, from the *Habanero* to the frigate *Esperanza.*

They were only given a few hours, allowing them to write down official statements and their goodbyes. They each pondered on their last thoughts and the words flowed on paper to their loved ones. At seven thirty, the order for the execution was signed by the Captain General. Ten prisoners completed their letters and statements at that time and the execution of Crittenden and his men was set for eleven o'clock the same morning.

With, "Not the heart to write to any of my family," Crittenden said, he sent one to a friend, saying his goodbyes and telling of the unjust and cruel treatment of his men by the Spanish. Then, just before the end, another letter he wrote and addressed to the Attorney

General of the United States, his uncle, John J. Crittenden.

Dear Uncle: In a few moments, some fifty of us will be shot. We came with López. You will do me the justice to believe that my motive was a good one. I was deceived by López – he, as well as the public press, assured me that the island was in a state of prosperous revolution.

I am commanded to finish writing at once. Your nephew, W.L. Crittenden

I will die like a man

Mr. Antonio Costa was given permission from the Spanish authorities to see the captured men on the *Esperanza*. He was a Spanish merchant, with houses in Havana and New Orleans. His loyalty was to Spain and the Spanish authorities had no doubt of his good intentions. Costa knew many of the men personally and tried to comfort them in their despair. Crittenden confided in Costa to have all the letters delivered to their friends and relatives back home.

At the time of the executions, Spanish guards came to get the prisoners and marched them down the ship's gangway, one by one. They had been stripped down to their trousers and shirts and some did not even have their shirts anymore. The Spanish admiral had, as prisoners, one colonel, three captains, four lieutenants, two surgeons, five sergeants and thirty-five soldiers. Crittenden was one of the last to leave the boat, following his men. He was stiff and slow in moving from being held captive in small quarters, and was told to be quick. As Crittenden walked, he was brutally struck in the face by a guard with the back of his hand. Crittenden returned the gesture by spitting back in the guard's face. The Spanish soldiers pulled and dragged the prisoners up the pathway. This walk would be the last for Crittenden and his men on the slope in front of Fort Atares.

The prisoners, including Crittenden, received the offenses charged against them. It was August 16th when the Spanish military court called the men "pirates" and hostile invaders of the island.

The men, chained together, were brought to the place of execution in a spectacle of brutality. They were brought before the firing squad, twelve at a time. Six were commanded to kneel, with their backs towards the firing squad standing about three paces away. Smoke filled the air when shots blasted at them as they fell to the ground. The next six prisoners, who had just witnessed their comrades being executed, were commanded to kneel opposite them and suffer the same misfortune.

When the moment of execution came for the officers, who were reserved for last, Crittenden and his officers were told to kneel with their backs to their executioners. They refused and said, "No!" followed by Captain Victor Kerr bravely adding, "We look death in the face!"

The Spanish officer of the execution ordered them again to kneel and Crittenden then replied, "An American kneels only to his God, and always faces his enemy." The men stood up proudly and faced their enemies. Adjutant R. C. Stanford, raised his head and shouted, "Cowards." Lieutenant Thomas James yelled,

"Our friends will avenge us! Liberty forever!" The last thing they heard was the crashing sound of musketry as they fell to the ground. Their bodies were riddled with bullets and started bleeding profusely. The gruesome scene of the execution of prisoners were witnessed by about twelve hundred Cuban citizens, including Spanish troops.

As they now lay dead on the ground bleeding from their wounds, the Spanish started beating their heads with the butt end of their muskets. The sounds of crushing skulls could be heard throughout the crowds as they cheered. Making these executions even worse, some of the Spanish officers brutally plunged their swords into the lifeless bodies of the gallant men, turning and twisting them around in their wounds as blood poured from their lifeless bodies. After the troops finished with their ghastly actions, they were ordered to withdraw. The bodies of the men were now passed over to the bloodthirsty mob, composed of the lowest and vilest of people, that was hired for discarding their bodies.

Both white and Creoles, from the city of Havana, spat on them, kicked and dragged them around by their heels as their bodies collected mud from the ground. Many of the bodies were mutilated in the most horrible and shocking manner. Any clothing that was left on the men were stripped, leaving them completely naked to desecrate them even more. Their blood was soaked into handkerchiefs attached to sticks, which were waved in celebration as they danced throughout the streets. The mob mutilated their limbs, tore out their eyes, cut off their noses, ears and fingers and some of the men had their private parts removed. Their fingers and skull fragments were nailed up throughout the city as a warning to others not to defy the Spanish government. What was left of their bodies was then carried away by the brutal, barbaric mob, who showcased them in the streets and public houses of the city on spikes and paraded them under the walls of the palace as if they were possessed.

The mob continued their sadistic evil until satisfied. Afterwards, the bodies were thrown naked, in their mutilated condition, six or seven at a time, into old hearses, haphazardly. These brave men were not allowed the use of coffins and were thrown into hearses that were used the year before for cholera victims and had not been cleaned since. The heads of the men were almost dragging on the ground and had the appearance of going to a slaughter house. With no respect for the dead, these men were piled on top of each other like carcasses of animals.

Being the "pirates," as they were called, there were no graves or consecrated ground for them to be buried in. The Spanish knew of only one solution. They were carted dishonorably to the heretic section of the old Espada cemetery. This section known as Potter's field was located just behind the San Lazaro hospital. They were thrown like dead animals into a muddy ditch where their bodies were covered with quicklime and hardly anything else. No ceremony or priest was there for the burial. The bodies of these courageous men were piled on top of one another, while the people cheered at their so-called victory.

By the maiming of the slaughtered dead and the indignity of the brutal burials for Crittenden and his men, the Spaniards violated the laws of humanity with their heinous acts. These courageous men died nobly, for a cause that was deemed sacred, with the inspirations of freedom for men. They now have the peace of a soldier, leaving the memory of men who died without fear and without dishonor.

Many Americans found it impossible to believe the mutilations of the dead bodies, when the news was printed in the papers across the United States. The publications explained the horrid trophies and sickening behavior as they exultingly exhibited in the public places of Havana. The atrocities of the Spanish were to be recognized in many cities.

Mr. A.F. Owens, the American Consul in Havana, did not make any attempt to see these unfortunate men in their last hours. He did not contact the Spanish Captain-General de la Concha to see if these men wanted to send any of their mementos to their loved ones. Some of the men had their wedding rings, watches and other personal items they may have wanted to send home. The families will have nothing from their fathers, brothers or sons... only their cherished memories.

Complaints against Mr. Owens, for his weak behavior towards the men who were set to die by the hands of the Spanish, were deep and menacing. He seemed to have no regard for those who were executed and their bodies thrown into ditches. Mr. Owens has said, "Oh, those men have been placed, by the President, beyond the pale of the law and I shall not interfere with them." He betrayed his country and humanity by absolutely refusing to plead for Crittenden and his men or to even visit them.

Antonio Costa gave solace to Crittenden and Kerr that he would do everything in his power to return their bodies. Costa spoke with the Captain General to obtain their bodies and he agreed. Costa kept his word and returned the bodies of Crittenden and Kerr back to the United States.

CHAPTER 9
MOUNTAIN ESCAPE

Before daybreak on the morning of the fifteenth, López and his men left the farmhouse and marched towards the mountains in the direction of Bahia Honda. The sun rose high in the sky and the heat was almost unbearable for the men. At ten o'clock they reached a coffee plantation in the valley below. It was surrounded by hills and just four miles south of Bahia Honda. This place was also entirely deserted, with no inhabitants to be found. López stationed the troops in the middle of the plantation, which was surrounded with high walls. Guards were stationed at the top of the walls in the direction of Bahia Honda, so they could observe the view in all directions in case of any movement that should arise from the Spanish. Here, the men killed some cattle and prepared a meal while resting once more.

A local Creole entered the walls of the plantation and asked for General López. He came to inform him that the Spanish troops were in strong force within Bahia Honda. He told López the Spanish had around twelve hundred infantry and approximately two hundred cavalry, along with the artillery. The Spanish knew of the location of General López and his filibusters at the plantation and planned to take possession of the road to the mountains at twelve o'clock noon, which López had planned to take with his men. They would attack with another division that same evening, which would come from the rear. General López consulted with his officers about the news and issued orders to immediately get the men ready to march. The order was given and the men assembled their packs and awaited their next assignment. Just before the march, General López took a few minutes to say a few words to his officers. He told them, "Set an example to the men in the cheerful endurance of fatigue and hardship".

William continues, "We advanced toward the mountains, expecting to find some insurgents there. As we had not found them on landing."

López believed it would be soon that they would unite with some insurgents waiting for them as he expected. These insurgents could take positions and help with the needed supplies. The officers told the men to stay together, but several had not heard this order and stayed behind. They would eventually be in the hands of the cruel Spanish troops who spared no one, whether they were armed or unarmed. The men started their march from the plantation around one o'clock in the afternoon. They marched swiftly with their Creole guide, who accompanied the friend who previously gave them the warning of the Spanish at Bahia Honda. The filibusters continued their march in the stifling hot sun. The packs they were carrying were beginning to be unbearable.

The men were now close to the mountains on a small

foot path that gradually ascended through the rocky terrain. The narrow path, with its tight enclosures and boulders, was blocked most of the way and made it very difficult for the men to keep up. Still they pressed on, trying to stay ahead of the Spanish troops who were close behind.

The night approached quickly and the men only had the stars to navigate through the mountains. Incredibly fatigued, they discovered a little house on top of the mountain, around eleven o'clock that night. Guards were posted again to keep a look out and the men were given a much-needed rest. The men did their best to seek comfort under trees and the open sky. Some used stones to rest their heads while others were consoled by the ground. The men had been without any food all that day and they could not find anything where they were that night. Their hunger pains ravaged their stomachs as they tried to rest, wondering what their next move would be.

Early the next day, on August 16th, the men awoke and continued to march into the mountains. They were faced with extremely rough, steep ascents and descents and became more exhausted with each passing minute. They came upon a plantation and stopped at around ten thirty that morning. They later learned the plantation was called Santa Maria. López recognized the owner, having known him years before when he lived on the island. He ordered the men to rest for a few hours, with the intention of continuing their march around four in the afternoon. The officers tended to their men, and guards were posted in case Spanish forces approached their position. The men were now without food for forty-eight hours and saw a couple of cattle on the plantation. The owner allowed the men to kill them and also provided plantains, along with corn, to cure their appetite. Tropical rains started to fall gently around them. They welcomed the rain, especially after the intense heat of the day. Some were able to wash their face and arms as the rain fell.

The men found a Creole nearby the plantation, who was hesitant when the filibusters approached him. The Creole was fully aware of the Spanish forces and the chance of being caught with López and his men would be disastrous for him. He confirmed the news of an insurrection in Pinar del Rio. He also said that the people of San Cristobal, on the countryside of the mountains, were ready to join López.

At around four o'clock that afternoon, after the men had a good meal and rested, López ordered the men to resume the march. Instead of the mountains, they witnessed the grandeur of hills and valleys filled with tropical vegetation. It seemed as though the men were walking near their homes instead of a country so much in turmoil. The men continued down the road towards San Cristobal when they came to a fork in the road. One direction was headed towards San Cristobal and the other to Bahia Honda. On this crossroad was a small farmhouse where they stopped. López found some cane brandy stored inside the farmhouse. He saw the men were low on moral and wanted to share this brandy with each of them. He had them line up as he poured each of them a moderate amount into their flask. As each weary man passed, he shook their hand and patted them on the shoulder, reassuring them with a simple nod of his head. An occasional word of English was spoken but the men knew the kindness he was showing to them. The men appreciated and acknowledged the generosity of the General. The men now could rest and enjoy their brandy in the solitude of the hills for the night.

López was still under the delusion that the Spanish troops were almost ready to come over and join him. On each encounter with the Spanish, he gave the signal to fire only with strong hesitation, fearing that he might have friends before him. López was not aware of the fate that happened earlier in the day to Crittenden and his men yet.

As the men rested for the night, they savored the fruits they were given earlier. Under the trees, they kept a watchful eye all evening as they tried to rest before the next day. The whole time they knew the Spanish troops could be in the immediate vicinity and could enter the camp they had made at any time.

CHAPTER 10
ATTACKED AT CAFETAL DE FRIAS

After a peaceful night, the next morning, on August 17th, they started their march in the direction of San Cristobal. López knew that if he continued down this road, it would eventually lead him to Cafetal de Frias, a coffee plantation which belonged to his wife's family. They saw the plantation in the distance and arrived at noon with the sun blazing down on them. López hoped to stay at Frias and remain for several days while the Spanish followed false leads in other directions. Twenty to thirty men were still unaccounted for by the time the filibusters reached Frias since leaving Las Pozas. They had fallen behind or fatigue overtook them and unfortunately they had probably fallen at the mercy of the Spanish troops. These men, along with others, were never seen again.

Arriving at Frias plantation, they hoped to receive a good meal and relax after their long, hot and humid day of marching. "We reached the plantation that had been formerly owned by López, and there his old slaves knelt to kiss his hands," said William. "The slaves brought us provisions and we camped under a big grove of mango trees with branches nearly touching the ground."

The Cafetal de Frias was settled on many acres with three large walls and with one side consisting of thick bushes and mango trees, enclosing the plantation. General López finally reached home, after many years of being away, and felt relieved and safe to be on his land again.

Around two o'clock in the afternoon, General López was resting inside the house when one of his guards gave the alarm of the presence of Spanish soldiers approaching. He quickly left the house and mounted his horse to patrol the location of his men in preparation for battle. The filibusters were resting under the mango trees on a hill when the guard alerted them of the Spanish nearby. The men hurried into their positions, getting ready to take aim.

William continues, "The men were exceedingly hungry, and were preparing dinner in all haste, when two or three squadrons of Spanish cavalry charged on us. Dinner was forgotten. We kept close in our shelter, but the branches of the trees kept the Spanish from getting close and we were firing all the time."

General Enna, the Spanish Commander in Chief and Second in Command on the island, was close to López's plantation with his troops. General Enna suspected that López would stop at the Frias plantation since he knew it was home to him. He knew it would be a good place to secure a trap for López and the filibusters. General Enna was prepared for battle, as he brought with him the Spanish cavalry, infantry and artillery.

The filibusters stayed hidden under the thick fringe of mango trees, strengthening their barrier with their large stems and dense foliage. This would be deemed difficult for horses to pass through and very useful for sharpshooters to take their aim against the Spanish. Shots were soon fired and the sharpshooters aim was effective on their targets.

General Enna stopped at the main house on the plantation and analyzed his position with the troops. López was deceived by the Spaniards once again, thinking they were intending to join him, and gave the word to the filibusters not to fire. Suddenly, General Enna ordered the charge! The filibusters aimed and shots were blasted through the air at the Spanish. The Spaniards were ultimately forced back, and many of the sharpshooters did not return the fire. They were still under orders from López to not shoot in case the troops were to join them.

The filibusters captured two of the Spanish advanced guards who were taken prisoner. Out of fear for their own lives, they let the filibusters know that the Spanish infantry was close behind them.

The Spanish force passed to the rear of the plantation with the intention of cutting off the retreat of the filibusters in case they escaped to the mountains. The filibusters quickly escaped to the foothills, which prevented them from being surrounded.

The Spaniards, with their early and quick firing, had missed the opportunity to stop the filibusters in their retreat. General Enna, while leading a flank attack, was mortally wounded in his stomach. The second-in-command decided to withdraw his Spanish infantry after learning about General Enna's demise. López's troops then charged the retreating Spaniards without effect and finding the Spaniards unlikely to return the fire. López shouted, "Hurray for the brave Americans! Three cheers for the Sons of Liberty!"

"They finally retreated with heavy losses. Prisoners we took said that they were the advanced guard of the 800 Spanish Infantry. At that news, we left our dinner and retreated along the road we had come, but we were met by the infantry. After fighting f o r fifteen minutes, the Spanish retreated. Among their dead was General Enna, second-in-command under General Concha," said William.

The filibusters captured the artillery as the Spanish cavalry were scattered to the right and left of the trees. The Spanish soldiers that were found dead or wounded, scattered throughout the plantation and under trees. They tried to help the suffering of the men, but with little medical supplies there was not much hope for the dying men. The filibusters gathered much needed supplies from the dead soldiers. López obtained a guide from his plantation at about two o'clock and the men resumed their march through a narrow footpath.

As the men headed towards the direction of San Cristobal, López again had hopes of finding insurgents where they were reported to be found. Lush vegetation and mango trees surrounded the men as they continued through the winding footpath. The wind started to pick up, giving relief to the filibusters from the long hot day.

They found another coffee plantation near the edge of the mountains where they stopped at about six o'clock that evening. The filibusters settled down and made camp for the night with a couple of cattle slaughtered for their supper. The rain started to fall that evening and lasted the entire night but at least the men had shelter to protect themselves.

The next morning, on August 18th, the light rain continued to fall as López gathered his men to continue their march towards San Cristobal. Most of the men were shoeless and walking barefoot, with mud above their ankles. Their swollen feet had deep cuts and bruises from the rugged terrain, making it almost unbearable to walk. General López and a couple of his officers rode ahead on horseback, while the men struggled on the descending path to keep up.

One by one, they made attempts to keep up with the others. They tried to help each other but the effort was getting too much even for one person to withstand. Those who could not endure the journey either collapsed or fell back from fatigue. The winds began to get stronger as the filibusters pushed forward, never giving up. As they passed a few farmhouses, the filibusters were received with kindness although the inhabitants had fear in their eyes. With exhaustion overwhelming the men, they rested in the corn fields nearby a farm house.

The Creoles at the farmhouse were worried that the news of the filibusters arriving at their homes would reach the Spanish authorities. López learned from one of the farmers there were about two thousand Spanish troops stationed in and around San Cristobal. William said, "After receiving the word of Crittenden's escape in the boats", López decided it was not the best way to go and therefore passed to the north of San Cristobal, going westward towards Pinar del Rio. The filibusters were discouraged having to retrace their steps, but they really had no choice if they did not want to encounter the Spanish.

CHAPTER 11
THE HURRICANE

Heavy rains began to descend on the men and their bodies were drenched. The gunpowder they were carrying was rendered useless. They turned back towards the path into the mountains where they reached a place called Candelaria. López believed this would be a safe haven for his men, thinking the Spanish would not follow. The officers inspected the troops and were surprised to find that half the men had dropped their muskets and left them behind. The ones who did have their muskets had little ammunition. Even though the rain continued to fall, the men could get some rest under trees.

In the early morning, on August 19th, the men gathered their supplies and climbed the narrow path with a steep ravine to their left. In the ravine, they noticed a cornfield that consumed the valley below. As the men struggled to keep their footing on the wet path, they heard the whistling of bullets coming from below. They knelt down to take cover behind boulders and trees nestled in the mountain. The Spanish found their position and aimed with deadly intent. With most of their muskets useless, only a few could return fire back at the enemy. López sped fast on his horse and past the men as he began using his machete to clear a path for his men to follow. Thick bushes divided them from the ravine as the Spanish troops continued their fire. The men quickly followed López, escaping the fire from the Spanish.

The rain steadily increased when they reached a narrow river with strong currents from the constant rainfall. The men had difficulty keeping together and slowly started separating from each other. As the men entered the river, it rose quickly with each increasing step as they walked from rock to rock, at times even up to their waist. A few of the men slipped into unforeseen holes and were engulfed to their neck. Unfortunately some of the men could not swim and, with the weight of their supplies, had to be helped by the other men. The Spanish soldiers seemed to have given up their pursuit to track and follow López and the filibusters. This may have been because of the increasing rain and no tracks to follow through the river. They finally reached the other side of the river and fell exhausted onto the banks.

Along the river's edge the men found palmetto trees as their only source of nourishment. They cut off the bark till they reached the heart. This was white and juicy and had a pleasant sweetness to the taste. It was similar to chewing on sugar cane. The men from the South had to show the others how to chew the hearts.

The men struggled to their feet and fought, with every step, against the gust of winds as the rain got stronger. Trees swayed back and forth wildly as branches fell from every direction. The rain and high winds were soon to get even worse. Huddling together under the trees, they shivered in the cold rain as it slammed against their bodies. They could not find any shelter and few still had clothing on their backs. The force from the sustained wind and rain felt like needles stinging their exposed skin. Heavy rain drained off the steep slopes like small waterfalls. The men hoped this night would soon be over, not realizing that a full force hurricane was heading straight for them.

It would be a long, cold and wet night for the filibusters. The suffering they experienced that night were indescribable. All the men could do was wait in the dark night until daybreak, hoping that their torment would come to an end. The massive storm they encountered was a hurricane named San Agapito. This destructive hurricane affected the entire Cuban island due to its large size with winds of one hundred and fifteen miles per hour. Every minute seemed like an hour with no protection in site.

The next morning (twentieth), López and his weary men walked aimlessly through the mountains. Some still had their guns, even though they were useless. Paths were now difficult to notice because of debris caused by the hurricane. Exhausted from starvation and loss of sleep, they could not find anything edible to eat. No fruits or palms could be found as they struggled to walk after their bodies were beaten down by the terrible storm. Their stiff bodies from the cold rains ached with every step to find their way out. They helped each other walk and barely carried anything on their backs except each other. Few of the men had never witnessed such winds and rains of this magnitude before.

The Spanish continued following them, but they found it increasingly difficult because of the storm. The filibusters tried to evade the Spanish as they made their way through the debris without the knowledge of the direction they were heading. The larger part of the men kept together and managed to make their way through the thick bushes, while a few of the men slowly lagged behind.

They saw a plantation that afternoon, in the distance, called Aguacate, and the rain and windy conditions continued as they made their way closer for shelter. The men hoped they could rest here and somehow dry their wet clothes. As evening approached, the men attempted to build fires which were deemed difficult. Everything around them was wet and there was nothing to burn. They settled down for the evening but still shivered, staying close to one another for warmth.

On the morning of the twenty-first, the rain finally stopped and the men started searching for food. The skies started to clear, the sun peaked out and raised the temperatures and humidity quickly. They advanced a few miles into a wild and uninhabited region as during the days before. With hunger and exhaustion tearing at their bodies, López ordered his horse to be killed so he could feed his men. William remembers, "At last, they were in such extremities that they killed General López's pony, which was fat, and ate it down to the last morsel—and needed another." This was the only food the men had for two long grueling days. With no dry wood found to make a fire, they gathered up anything they could find that would burn. The men gathered any paper, stocks of broken muskets and as much dry powder that could be found. Without the will to give up, a fire was soon started. They ate everything on the horse and still wanted more. After days of not eating, about one hundred and sixty men made a meal of General López's horse.

CHAPTER 12
NEW ORLEANS RIOTS

The U.S. mail steamer *Empire City*, commanded by John Tanner, left Havana on the evening of August 18th and arrived in New Orleans on the morning of the twenty-first. Soon after she docked, people learned that she brought the tragic news of the barbaric executions in Havana. The steamer *Crescent City* also arrived that same morning with Mr. Brincio, the Secretary of the Spanish Consulate. He was entrusted by the Captain, General Concha, with the handwritten letters of the last words from Crittenden and his men to be delivered to their loved ones.

The Spanish Consulate obtained possession of these sacred letters and he declined forwarding them to the State Department at Washington, D.C. This was the proper protocol of the effects of persons dying abroad. Some of the citizens went to the Consulate and could receive their letters. However, a rumor spread throughout the city that the Consul refused to deliver the letters or bring them to the post office. Upon hearing the disruption of the people, the Secretary of the Spanish Consulate immediately went to the post office with the remaining letters and deposited them. The letters were deposited at three thirty that afternoon. Unfortunately, the citizens had begun to take matters into their own hands, not knowing that the letters were already at the post office.

The newspaper called *La Unión*, a local New Orleans Spanish newspaper, printed an article prior to hearing the news of Crittenden and his men being executed. The article below was considered very offensive and improper character towards Americans.

"Much is said about the stringency of the laws of that island, but the restrictions bear only upon the bad; and the good part of the population enjoys more liberty now than it would, if the island should be annexed to the United States. We, during our many years residence on the island, enjoyed more liberty than we ever did in New Orleans; for here, there is no liberty of speech, one must hurrah with the crowd, or give offense and expose oneself to all manner of insult. Here, one must sing to the praise and glory of the place in which he is, or keep silent as a slave. In spite of all the boast of liberty made here, it is very one-sided, existing in theory; and in all parts we see exhibited all the intolerance of the Puritans, who fled from persecution in Europe to persecute in America. The Cubans are a polite people, and in their manners are more refined than the Americans, whose awkwardness and grossness shock them; and, as for those persons who go about drinking places and roar out abuse, they are considered as perfect barbarians; something below the Congo race. It happens too, often, that Americans tell foreigners that they are slaves, or say something offensive in regard to their country, without appearing to consider that they are insulting those individuals; but the Americans are so sensitive themselves that a mere allusion in a favorable tone, to anything in another country, sounds, in the ear of the American, as against a similar object in his own country. Therefore, people of dispositions and tastes so different could never agree, and the poor Cubans, being the weakest, would go to the wall."

During the morning after the news arrived about the executions in Havana, placards were posted throughout the city threatening the newspaper office of *La Unión*. The citizens had planned to attack the newspaper that evening, letting everyone know the anger of the insulting words *La Unión* had been saying about Americans.

The Spanish press became aware of the placards placed all over the city. The angry press retaliated by issuing the following article:

"New Orleans papers, there is your work! There is the result of your derogations, of your iniquitous falsehoods, of your placards with large black letters, and your detestable extras. There you have that scattered blood and that will be scattered in future. There you have it, smoking in accusation against you, perverse instigators, against you, who have murdered those deluded men, whom you have sent to death – for you knew well that they certainly would be killed. This blood must flow, drop by drop, upon your heads — this blood will torment you in your sleep, for they have lost their lives when you were in security in your houses."

A mob immediately formed and divided into groups. Their target was to destroy all Spanish owned establishments. The city authorities could do little to restrain the chaos within the streets. The owners and men who worked for the Spanish businesses were suspected of being spies. Many thought they were working secretly for Juan Laborde, Spanish Consul in New Orleans. The Spanish Consulate was located on Bourbon Street near the corner of St. Louis Street. Rioters felt these spies tried to destroy their efforts to liberate Cuba in the López Expedition. They also thought the Spanish citizens would again inform authorities of the Consulate of any other future plans.

Local merchants objected to the stores owned by the Spanish, where they sold smuggled cigars from Cuba at lower prices. The Spanish merchants avoided paying import duties on their merchandise. Spanish coffee house owners usually got away without paying city taxes by bribing the local law authorities.

New Orleans was the scene of outrageous disturbances. Angry crowds grew and filled the cobble stone streets as they demonstrated through the city in search of businesses owned only by the Spanish. The uncontrollable mob carried pipes, sticks and anything else that would be found with the intent to destroy. Their first target was the fruit and vegetable stands at the local markets. The outraged citizens proceeded to demolish the fruit and vegetable stands – not only because they were Spanish, but for monopolizing the city's fruit trade with their high cost.

The paper *La Unión* was the particular object of resentment. As a consequence of its harsh language toward Americans and from its 'Extra,' announcing the Spanish triumph. The people of New Orleans were infuriated. The Spanish citizens used offensive language and rejoiced over their fate to the rioters, only making things worse. Americans in New Orleans did not want derogatory statements to be heard after hearing the fate of these unfortunate men who joined the expedition. The paper had been threatened with an attack in the evening but the raiding took place between two and three o'clock in the afternoon. A crowd entered the *La Unión* building on Exchange Alley below Conti Street. Several hundred men of upper class backgrounds initiated the assault on the newspaper office and physically participated in its destruction. They destroyed the forms and presses and most all of the *La Unión's* contents. Everything in the building was pulled out onto the street and destroyed, including the type.

They began breaking into the cigar and liquor shops, gutting them of their contents and destroying everything they could lay their hands upon. The cigar shop, "La Corina," located on the corner of St. Charles Avenue and Gravier Street, was approached by the mob. This shop was owned by a Spaniard they detested, Don Francisco Remagassa. The men tried to push open the doors but it remained locked. After an hour of beating and pounding on the door, Remagassa appeared, armed with a drawn dagger in his hand. He shouted, with the intent to harm the rioters if they proceeded any further. Mr. B. Gonzales, an employee of the cigar shop, shouted loudly over the Havana massacre. He rushed into the crowd with his drawn dirk and wounded three, one severely. Remagassa barely made his escape into the store, closing the door after him. The rioters pushed their way through the door and began destroying everything inside. Remagassa fled out the back of the store into the alley, barely escaping with his life. Blood was streaming from his face as the men hurled stones at his getaway. He soon found refuge in the city prison. Mr. Gonzales was arrested later for his cruel acts.

The mob had already begun to vandalize the coffee house at the corner of Poydras Street and Tchoupitoulas Street when the Mayor of New Orleans, Abdiel Crossman, arrived. He spoke with the rioters and told them to "Respect the Law."

The Jenny Lind coffee house, located at the corner of St. Charles Avenue and Perdido Street, was destroyed. The Piny Woods coffee house near the New Basin Canal was also destroyed. The exquisite cigar store, owned by Don Y. M. Caballero, located on Royal Street, Customhouse and Fernandez on Royal Street, under the St. Louis Hotel, were also victims of the rioters. The mob continued to search for businesses owned by Spanish citizens and destroyed them.

During the same afternoon, between five and six o'clock, the office of the Spanish Consulate was attacked. The rioters forced their way through the doors of the building and commenced to destroy its contents. J.

Genois, Recorder of the First Municipality, arrived at the Consulate at the same time as the destruction was taking place. Police officers arrived with him and commanded the rioters to stop at once. The rioters were able to obtain the Consul's sign as they withdrew from the building. The doors were nailed shut by the authorities. The angry mob took the Consul's sign and it was brought to the public square to be burned for everyone to witness. The rioters returned back to the Consulate about an hour later and forced their way through the doors to continue their wrath. Angrily, they threw the archives of the Consulate into the street and defaced the portraits of the Queen of Spain and the Captain-General of Cuba. The Spanish flag was torn into shreds and scattered throughout the building.

Mayor Crossman called for an assembly for the citizens to attend at Lafayette Square that evening at eight o'clock. A massive crowd gathered, almost two hours before the scheduled time.

This meeting was addressed by Mayor Crossman, M.M. Reynolds the District Attorney for New Orleans, Judge Walker, Colonel C.R. Wheat and Colonel Field of the Louisiana Regiment. Judge Walker spoke loudly at the crowd and advised them to "Bottle their wrath for use in Cuba."

When the time came for Colonel Wheat to speak, his concerns about Crittenden and the men who were executed were addressed. He calmly said, "Were I to die this moment, I would have the proud satisfaction of knowing that I leave others behind to prosecute the good cause, and I would join the spirits of the gallant Crittenden and his companions in the land of dreams." The mayor then addressed the crowd and tried to calm them down with counseling mediation, but with no avail.

When the meeting was coming to a close, the outbreak of the riots rapidly increased after the mayor's speech. The public authorities were not prepared when people started shouting, "White Hall", a coffee shop located across from the St. Louis Hotel. Hundreds of people rushed in that direction and along the way on Exchange Alley more Spanish shops were broken into and vandalized.

There was a proclamation by the mayor: Mayoralty of New Orleans, August 21, 1851, 11.00 p.m.:

"Whereas, during this afternoon and night, certain persons have so far forgotten the obedience due to the laws of their country, as to openly violate the place by creating riots and disturbances, which unfortunately for the good reputation of the city, have terminated in the destruction of property and, whereas it is essential to the well-being of society that the supremacy of the laws be maintained, I, A.D. Crossman, Mayor of the City of New Orleans, therefore issue this my proclamation, calling on all good citizens to aid in suppressing these disturbances, and to assist the authorities in preserving the order, peace, and dignity of the city."

-A.D. Crossman, Mayor

Though the Spanish riots of New Orleans on Thursday, August 21st in 1851, there was very little bloodshed and no deaths. In total, seventeen Spanish establishments, twelve coffeehouses and five cigar stores, *La Unión* newspaper and Spanish consulate were destroyed by the rioters. Some Spanish citizens in fear of their lives, left New Orleans at the end of August. Nearly two hundred Spanish citizens, approximately ten percent of the Spanish population fled the city.

Close to midnight, a large crowd of rioters gathered at the corner of Julia Street and Magazine Street. They were in the midst of destruction when the authorities arrived on the scene and arrested forty people. Police gathered the men and brought them before Judge Alderman Hawthorne. Only thirty-three men were delivered to the First District Court of New Orleans. They were tried on, "Engaged in a riot, destroying property and endangering the lives of the citizens." Not one 'Cuba Emigrant' was arrested that night.

The next day, August 22nd, the schooner, *Fairy*, arrived in New Orleans from Cuba with the bodies of Colonel William Logan Crittenden, Captain Victor Kerr and Lieutenant James Brandt. Hundreds gathered by the dock to witness the somber site as the bodies were taken off the ship. Heads were bowed and whispers of prayers could be heard as the bodies were placed into waiting horse-drawn hearses and given the upmost respect.

Many cities in the United States heard about the riots that took place in New Orleans. Hundreds of rumors circulated as people gathered, with feelings of horror and indignation towards Spain increasing. They wanted to show their compassion for the Cuban filibusters and to protest against the conduct of Spain. In Philadelphia, crowds assembled in the streets, totaling near twelve thousand. The meeting was conducted by an ex-mayor proclaiming resolutions to be adopted. The resolution stipulated that, "The United States should propose to Spain immediate autonomy for Cuba. In case war should result from this ultimatum, the United States should continue to fight until Cuba was independent." Other places, like Savannah, Mobile, Cincinnati, Baltimore, Louisville and Pittsburgh, had similar protests, with large crowds, in sympathy for the filibusters. A newspaper in New York said that a crowd of four thousand people gathered in the streets. Later that evening, a procession was held and was to contain as many as fifteen thousand people.

The news received was described in the papers of the following days: "Oaths of eternal hatred for the Spanish domination, and of unappeasable revenge, were uttered by many lips not ordinarily given to speak under excitement. Verily, if Havana had been within reach yesterday, the walls of the city would have been torn down with naked hands, rather than such a piece of bloodthirsty cruelty should have gone without instant punishment."

CHAPTER 13
FILIBUSTERS HAVE SECOND THOUGHTS

The next day, on the twenty-second, the filibusters and a few of the officers had enough of traveling through mountains and valleys leading nowhere. They went to General López and explained they could not endure the sufferings any longer and demanded to return to the United States. The filibusters felt they were going in circles and they were misled when they realized the people of Cuba did not support them in their expedition. There were no military reinforcements on the island to help in their purpose of liberating Cuba. They stood before the General and demanded he should abandon the expedition and to take them back to the coast. Once there, they hoped to find small vessels to help with their escape from the island. López did not want to fight with his men knowing the disappointment he had caused them. He decided to descend the next day to the plains to collect the much-needed supplies and provisions. López wanted to return to the mountains with his men and stay hidden so the Spanish would not attack them.

López told the filibusters and the officers, "If, after that, no change should take place in their situation within ten days, he would then release all from any obligation or pledge to remain with him any longer to share his fate, and they might make the best attempt that the situation permitted to get back to the United States." López did not want to go back with the men to the United States. He would rather die in his beloved Cuba or see Cuba free.

The men agreed and gathered their packs and began their march hopefully one last time. The next morning, the men descended from the mountains to the valley to look for food. The skies were clear and the sun warmed their faces. By noon, the men still had not eaten anything. They slowly returned into the mountains, always aware of Spanish troops in the area. These men were in a hostile country without food, ammunition that was useless and led by a Cuban with no help in sight. Starvation gripped at their souls and fatigue overwhelmed every inch of their bodies. The night was humid and hot as it was during the day and the men fell into an exhaustive sleep.

The twenty-fourth, the filibusters descended from the mountains again until they reached a road from Bahia Honda to San Cristobal. They continued on this road until the early evening, when two Spanish guards were noticed on the road. The guards quickly escaped from their presence. It was a probability that they might be advanced guards of the Spanish troops in the area. An immediate halt was ordered to inspect what was left of their weapons and ammunition.

The men were shaken and knew an attack would be imminent. As expected, a force of almost nine hundred

Spanish troops were ready to ambush the filibusters just some four hundred yards away. The tremor of horses was felt beneath their feet as the men scattered into small groups, reaching for escape in the mountains. Guns and supplies were strewn throughout their path hoping to lessen their weight for a quick retreat.

Unfortunately, many of the men were defenseless against the slaughter of the Spanish troops. Cries and moans could be heard from a distance as no mercy was shown for these brave men. General López was separated from most of the men who had courageously joined him for his expedition and had only seven who remained with him.

William was able to get away from the slaughter of the Spanish and fled to the mountains. He said, "In the retreat it was every man for himself and the band was scattered". One can only think of what these men were going through. Everything was against them from the start of the expedition, including that they were only equipped with old flint-lock rifles while the Spanish guns had new percussion locks. Their hopes for liberating Cuba from Spain was far from their thoughts and military jurisdiction was forgotten. The remaining filibusters were only surviving at this point in time, and trying to stay alive.

By the twenty-sixth, the men were wandering around the mountains not knowing their whereabouts. With their bodies emaciated and weary and having barely enough strength to walk, they left the mountains and headed for the plains. They considered it would be better to be shot and killed by the Spanish than to die a slow death of starvation. As they descended, water was found between the hollows of rocks and on top of leaves to moisten their lips. The strength and care for life was slowing escaping their souls.

Through winding paths ahead, and with great exertion, they quickly went into the valley hoping to find food and water. They saw a house in the distance and decided to approach with caution. When they arrived, they were treated with a great deal of kindness and were given much needed food. The men were thankful for the kindness and filled their stomachs with fruit and fresh water. The farmer of the house m a d e arrangements to secure a guide for the filibusters. He said the guide would lead them to the coast, with provisions and supplies. The men finally had hopes of leaving their nightmare on the island.

After the provisions were secured, they took cover and rested till nightfall. They made plans to go to the coast that night when everything was clear. They were unaware of the large number of countrymen hiding and waiting to make their ambush on these filibusters. The men were largely outnumbered and were not prepared for a battle. They were surrounded and the filibusters knew their quest had now come to an end. They were taken prisoner and their hands were tightly bound together as they were led to San Cristobal.

William, luckily, was not one of those men who were captured. "Myself and five others," says William, "kept on for a day or two, eating wild fruit. We saw a house in a valley, and were so hungry and desperate that we risked going to it. We were welcomed by the inmates, as one of our party spoke Spanish. We got a fine meal and the promise of a guide to the nearest seashore in the morning. We thought that if we could reach the coast we might find a boat and get away from the country. In the morning, we started with the promised guide. In a few hours he led us straight into the Spanish camp. Of course, we were captured, disarmed, and they led us into a small town and put us into a cell where we found ten or twelve of our other men. Information was posted throughout the woods everywhere that if we gave ourselves up we would be sent back to the United States."

William reflected on that grave day as he started to lose hope. "In the morning, we were marched out again and told we were going to be shot. They took us to a cleared place where a number of graves had been made and there were the shirts and hats of our men on the graves. We were drawn up in line, they raised their guns and then we were ordered on the march again. It had just been one of their grim jokes." The Spanish teased and provoked the men as they made them walk to the shoreline. William continued, "We were taken to the seashore and there put into an old hulk and kept for two days, when we were transferred to a steamer and taken to Havana."

CHAPTER 14
LÓPEZ CAPTURED

López separated from his men, and only his loyal body servant, Pedro, stayed faithfully with him. Pedro Manuel López was his nephew, a mulatto, and had been by his side since they left New Orleans. They continued closer into the mountains, hoping to escape the grasp of the Spanish. Time was running out for López and he knew the Spanish soldiers were closing in on him. They stayed hidden in the bushes and trees as their canopy of safety.

A group of Creoles, led by a peasant, Don Antonio Santos Castaneda, were in pursuit of López. Their thirsty bloodhounds picked up the scent quickly and ran ahead some distance. When the bloodhounds finally caught up with López, they savagely held onto his left leg preventing him from escaping. As their teeth sunk into his flesh, López tried to get away but their jaws tightened as they held onto his bloodied and torn pantaloons. The Creoles reached López and released the bloodhounds from their grip. López scarcely had the strength to stand when he was finally captured. They bound his hands together tightly and wrapped a rope around his neck as they pulled him along the path. López was near exhaustion from fatigue and hunger. He was captured near San Cristobal, in Pinos de Raguel, on the morning of August 29th. López realized his fate was now in the hands of the Creoles who had every intention to turn him over to the Spanish authorities.

General López was immediately brought to San Cristobal. The men pulled on the rope as López was pulled through the streets and he received insulting screams as he approached the town. The Spanish troops heavily guarded López, isolating him from the other prisoners. The Spanish officer in command made plans to relocate López, without any delay, in a precautionary manner. The officer chose the intended route, but sent López by another route in an expedited march in secrecy.

López arrived at the Port of Mariel, approximately twenty-five miles west of Havana and boarded the steamer *Almendares*. He was kept separate from the other captured prisoners, including William, who were in iron chains and corralled together. William said, "We were taken to the seashore, put into an old hulk and kept for two days, after which we were transferred to a steamer and taken to Havana."

The steamer was delayed, waiting for López and at two o'clock he boarded the *Almendares*. Hours later, after given word from Spanish authorities, López was then transferred to the steamer *Pizarro,* while William and the other prisoners headed for Havana on the *Almendares*. López was treated fairly and given a cigar while in captivity. He was able to walk freely on the ship while still being heavily guarded by the Spanish military. López pleasantly spoke with the guards who still respected him as their general and not a prisoner. The

Pizarro stayed anchored outside the port of Mariel until they received word from Spanish authorities to proceed to Havana with López. Once word was given, the Spanish brought López to Havana and docked on the thirty-first.

William arrived in Havana with the other filibusters. He said, "We spent the first two days in Morro Castle and were then taken to La Cabana, another prison, where we found fifty or sixty of our men." The men were pushed through a crude process when they arrived at the prison. They were sent in single file to have their heads shaved and then to another to have their facial hair removed. Prison uniforms were issued to them as the men stayed securely fastened together in chains. As they walked in pairs the weight of the chain, similar to a log chain, was increasingly difficult with each step.

William remembers, after two days in prison, "We heard music and shouting outside and when we asked the sentries what was going on – for we could not see – they told us that they were garroting López." Garroting is a method of capital punishment of Spanish origin. A prisoner is placed on a stool as an executioner places an iron collar around a condemned person's neck – then the collar is tightened by a crank until death occurs by strangulation. In this case, injury to the spinal column occurs at the base of the brain when a screw enters from behind, causing instant death. The Spanish wanted to garrote López because they felt he was not deserving of the death of a soldier by simply being shot.

Early in the morning, the Spanish military came to

the ship and escorted López to La Punta. Under heavy guard, López was led through the people waiting on shore to see the General walk down the gangway.

Just before seven in the morning, William and the other prisoners were brought out of their prison cells at Morro Castle. Their hands quickly covered their eyes from the scorching sunlight after leaving their darkened cells. The Spanish guards positioned them on the upper walls of the Morro, looking across a very narrow channel into La Punta plaza. As they were still chained together, the Spanish wanted the prisoners to witness for themselves the garroting of their leader, General Narsico López.

The news of López's capture and his anticipated garroting spread quickly throughout the island. The plaza filled with Spanish military consisting of three thousand infantry and two thousand cavalry. Huddled masses of citizens, approximately twenty thousand, went to witness the last moments of López. People also stood on the balconies above and consumed the entire area surrounding the plaza where López was to be garroted.

A scaffold had been built in the center of the plaza reaching about ten feet high above the multitude of commoners. In the middle of the platform was a solid wooden post, fourteen inches in width. It rose through the platform five feet high with a small stool against the post that awaited for López. A railing surrounded the scaffold enclosing the platform with only a few small steps leading up to his demise.

The soldiers surrounded López as his hands were

tightly bound together in front of him. He started walking slowly with his head held high. A white cloak covered his head and the military uniform he wore in the expedition. The guards led him through the hostile crowds until he reached the scaffold. Priests stood on both sides of López, wearing long black caps and carrying a black banner as he walked slowly through the plaza. The black executioner walked before him, leading the way.

The crowd shouted angrily with cheers as López walked up the steps to the platform. López looked upon the preparations for his death and his facial expressions did not change. One can only wonder what he must have been thinking as he stood on the platform facing the people of his beloved Cuba. Reaching the platform, the executioner removed his cloak and everyone saw that López was still in his embroidered full-dress military uniform. He wore his cravat, sash and all of the insignia of his military rank he had achieved. His appearance was calm and dignified as he stood in front of the vast assemblage of people. The executioner then removed his embroidered coat to show even more disgrace to the General. An officer on the platform shouted loudly and demanded complete silence from the people. In an instant the crowd looked upon the officer and quiet whispers was all that was left.

With the priest, now at his side, and the executioner on the other, López spoke for a few minutes concluding with these words: "I pray the persons who have compromised me to pardon me as I pardon them. My death will not change the destinies of Cuba."

Standing close behind him, the executioner interrupted López in an offensive tone and said, "Come, be quick, be quick."

López quickly sneered at him, while gritting his teeth, as he said, "Wait sir." Then he continued and said, "Adieu, my beloved Cuba. Adieu, my brethren."

López stared at the crowd as he bowed his head. He took his seat on the stool and eased his head back. The executioner placed the cold iron collar securely around his neck and his feet were then bound to the sides of the stool. López's heart was racing as he felt the cold steel against his neck; still, his expression did not change. The priest gave López a crucifix to hold in his hour of mercy. Just as he leaned over to kiss the sacred cross, the executioner then slowly started to turn the crank tightening the iron collar. There was a second turn, and the people witnessed silently as, at the last turn, the screw penetrated through the back of his neck, piercing his spinal cord. His eyes became large as he tried to gasp for his last breath of air, then his head slumped forward. No applause or shouting could be heard. It was fifteen minutes past seven in the morning, on September 1, 1851, when López took his last breath. After the execution, López's body was taken from the garrote and was given a private burial.

His three year campaign to liberate Cuba from the tyranny of Spain came to an unexpected and abrupt end. Immediately after his execution, the seventeen Creoles who captured López were each publicly presented one thousand dollars along with the cross of honor from the Spanish officials.

During his campaigns, López designed a banner that was carried throughout his expeditions. This banner became the flag of Cuba on May 20, 1902 and still stands today as their national flag. The colors of the Cuban banner, through López's eyes, are three blue bands which stand for the three military districts of Colonial Cuba, two white stripes are for the purity of the patriotic cause and the red symbolizes the bloodshed in the struggle for independence. The white star represents unity. The triangle is for equality, strength and brotherhood.

The executions of López and Crittenden with his men, caused outrage in both the northern and southern United States. Many who did not support the expedition, found the Spanish treatment of the prisoners brutal and inhumane.

General López could have profoundly altered politics in the United States, giving a strong Caribbean foothold, if he had succeeded. This could have triggered further expansion of the United States. Instead, the failure of López with the filibusters discouraged Americans, especially in the South. The fault may have been on López for his separation from Crittenden. They should have stayed together and fought together. Leaving behind the artillery and the best men with Crittenden was disastrous. If Crittenden would have reached López, the outcome of the expedition could have been different. López's death spelled the end of any future expeditions to Cuba.

CHAPTER 15
IMPRISONMENT FOR WILLIAM COUSANS

After López's death, the prisoners did not know what was to become of their fate. During their imprisonment, the American Consul, Mr Owens, seemed to have done nothing to help them. The British Consul, Joseph T. Crawford, did, however, try to visit the prisoners as a private citizen, but to no avail. He was denied entrance – then went back wearing his military uniform and demanded admittance. He would stand before them and not back down, insisting he wanted to see the prisoners. The prison guards were then obliged to allow him to enter. The prisoners were told by the British Consul that it was the intention of the authorities to send the prisoners to Central America. William and the others were relieved that they would not be executed. The British consul continued to come, day after day, bringing tobacco to the men, wrote letters to their loved ones, and showed them respect. Mr. Owens finally showed himself on the last day but was not welcomed by the prisoners and quickly thrown out of the prison.

Captain General Concha stated that he would have pardoned all the prisoners if it had not been for the riots that took place in New Orleans against the Spanish citizens and their businesses. Captain Charles T. Platt, Commander of the United States ship *Albany*, pleaded for the release of the prisoners. He learned it was determined that the prisoners would be sent to Spain. *Albany* was in the Gulf waters to prevent any more filibuster expeditions entering Cuban territory and was docked in Havana Bay when Crittenden and his men were brought to Fort Atares for their executions.

William and the prisoners finally had heard of their fate and what was to become of them. They were to be sentenced as a chain-gang to ten years' hard labor in the quicksilver mines in Spain. A few ships were to transport these prisoners at different times.

The following letter is from the prisoners at Havana, Havana city prison September 7, 1851:

"We, the undersigned officers and men, now incarcerated in the city prison of Havana on account of our participation in the late expedition against the island of Cuba, under the command of Gen. López, and being about to embark for Spain, cannot refrain from expressing our heartfelt gratitude to Joseph T. Crawford, Consul-General of her Britannic Majesty, and to Mr. W. Sydney Smith, British Consulate at this place. To Mr. J.S. Thrasher and to the American and British citizens of Havana generally, we also owe a debt of deep and lasting gratitude. To them we owe all, for, by their kindness and generosity, we have been enabled to overcome many of the difficulties and sufferings we should have otherwise undergone. To them we owe a debt of gratitude we would willingly express in words, but language fails us. Hoping, however, that, should we be spared to return to our homes, we may have an opportunity of repaying, in part, the debt we owe. Should such not be the case, we sincerely pray that God, the Ruler of the Universe, and lover of good acts, may repay them by bestowing upon them, in this world, all the blessings that a Divine Providence can bestow, and after death, by a reward more lasting still, life eternal.

Signed:

Major Louis Schlessinger Capt. R.M. Grider

Lt. Edmund H. McDonald Capt. R. H. Ellis

Lt. David Winborn, and 133 others"

A letter from Jefferson Davis explains his concern for the prisoners of the López Expedition:

"Our flag has been wantonly insulted in the Caribbean sea... captured citizens of our country [were] sent in a slave ship to the coast of Spain, fettered, according to the custom of that inhuman traffic, and released, not as an acknowledgement of wrong on demand of our government, but as a gracious boon accorded to a friendly suit. Whilst the dying words of Crittenden yet rung in the American ear, and the heart turned, sickening, away from the mutilated remains of his liberty-loving followers; whilst public indignation yet swelled at the torture which had been inflicted on our captive countrymen, even then we were called upon to witness a further manifestation of the truckling spirit of the administration..."

CHAPTER 16
PRISONERS' VOYAGE TO SPAIN

The prisoners' chains were removed on Sunday morning, September 7th, and they were allowed to bathe. They were in good spirits and given writing materials, at the request of W. Sidney Smith, secretary to the British Consul, to send letters home to their loved ones. Many tireless people contributed money or their services to help these men while they were in prison. On the next day, the prisoners were removed from their prison cell during the night to get ready for their departure early in the morning. They were each assigned a pea jacket, a woolen shirt, a pair of pants, a pair of stockings and a tin pot. The men were led to the dock but, before their departure, they were given bread and coffee.

William said, "After nine days, the prisoners were removed in the night and taken to the transport *Guatemala*, an old slave ship, which started for Spain." The prisoners left in good spirits and it was whispered among them that they would be pardoned soon after reaching Ceuta. William continues, "The men were stowed away between decks and were kept in irons for three weeks of the voyage, suffering inconceivable tortures from the heat and foul air. The only light or ventilation was from the lattice over the hatchway, where guards watched constantly. The food was horrible."

The *Primera de Guatemala* started her long voyage on September 8th and was escorted by a gunboat, the Spanish war sloop *Venus*. Even though the prisoners were in chains, escape would be impossible for them. Three steamers sailed from Havana with the remaining prisoners a few weeks later.

The *Guatemala* carried most of the prisoners for the journey across the open Atlantic Ocean. The long voyage was deemed treacherous. She spread her sails to the ocean winds and faced rough seas, as many of the prisoners fell ill from dysentery. At night, the prisoners were fastened to their berths with an iron ring attached to their ankle. The torture must have been devastating for these young men. The meals were completely insufficient. Although they were allowed on board for necessary reasons, they occasionally assisted in helping the seamen with their work.

It took nearly two months to cross the rough seas of the Atlantic Ocean. The first stop was at Ceuta for fortifications at the prison. Ceuta stands on a small peninsula that reaches out into the Mediterranean Sea from the coast of North Africa. This was Spain's penal colony, a seaport of Africa, belonging to Spain. Located in Morocco, it is opposite of Gibraltar. The castle occupied one of the highest points on a mountain.

The men did not stay long in Ceuta and proceeded to the harbor of Cadiz, Spain, and stayed for three days. They were then ordered away to quarantine at Vigo,

Spain. When they arrived, they were to stay in an old castle on the Bay of Vigo. The men were glad to put their feet upon solid ground, although they were still in chains but able to breathe fresh air again. After weeks of quarantine the men were placed back on the *Guatemala* and brought ashore to the mainland of Vigo along with two vessels, *Venus* and *Isabella Catolica,* carrying more of the filibusters.

President Millard Fillmore, the thirteenth President of the United States, delivered the State of the Union Address, informing Congress of the López Expedition and prisoners, dated December 2, 1851.

"Since the close of the last Congress certain Cubans and other foreigners resident in the United States, who were more or less concerned in the previous invasion of Cuba, instead of being discouraged by its failure, have again abused the hospitality of this country by making it the scene of the equipment of another military expedition against that possession of Her Catholic Majesty, in which they were countenanced, aided, and joined by citizens of the United States. On receiving intelligence that such designs were entertained, I lost no time in issuing such instructions to the proper officers of the United States as seemed to be called for by the occasion. By the proclamation, a copy of which is herewith submitted I also warned those, who might be in danger of being inveigled into this scheme, of its unlawful character and of the penalties which they would incur. For some time, there was reason to hope that these measures had sufficed to prevent any such attempt. This hope, however, proved to be delusive. Very early in the morning of the third of August a steamer called the *Pampero* departed from New Orleans for Cuba, having on board upward of 400 armed men with evident intentions to make war upon the authorities of the island. This expedition was set on foot in palpable violation of the laws of the United States. Its leader was a Spaniard, and several of the chief officers and some others engaged in it were foreigners. The persons composing it, however, were mostly citizens of the United States.

Before the expedition set out, and probably before it was organized, a slight insurrectionary movement, which appears to have been soon suppressed, had taken place in the eastern quarter of Cuba. The importance of this movement was, unfortunately, so much exaggerated in the accounts of it published in this country, that these adventurers seem to have been led to believe that the Creole population of the island not only desired to throw off the authority of the mother country, but had resolved upon that step and had begun a well-concerted enterprise for effecting it. The persons engaged in the expedition were generally young and ill-informed. The steamer in which they embarked left New Orleans stealthily and without a clearance. After touching at Key West, she proceeded to the coast of Cuba and, on the night between the 11th and 12th of August, landed the persons on board at Playtas, within about twenty leagues of Havana.

The main body of them proceeded to, and took possession of, an inland village six leagues distant, leaving others to follow in charge of the baggage as soon as the means of transportation could be obtained. The latter, having taken up their line of march to connect themselves with the main body, and having proceeded about four leagues into the country, were attacked on the morning of the thirteenth by a body of Spanish troops and a bloody conflict ensued, after which they retreated to the place of disembarkation, where about fifty of them obtained boats and re-embarked therein. They were, however, intercepted among the keys near the shore by a Spanish steamer cruising on the coast, captured and carried to Havana and, after being examined before a military court, were sentenced to be publicly executed – and the sentence was carried into effect on the August 16.

On receiving information of what had occurred, Commodore Foxhall A. Parker was instructed to proceed in the steam frigate, *Saranac,* to Havana and inquire into the charges against the persons executed, the circumstances under which they were taken and whatsoever referred to their trial and sentence. Copies of the instructions from the Department of State to him and of his letters to that Department are herewith submitted.

According to the record of the examination, the prisoners all admitted the offenses charged against them… of being hostile invaders of the island. At the time of their trial and execution, the main body of the invaders was still in the field making war upon the Spanish authorities and Spanish subjects. After the lapse of some days, being overcome by the Spanish troops, they dispersed on August 24. López, their leader, was captured some days after and executed on September 1. Many of his remaining followers were killed or died of hunger and fatigue and the rest were made prisoners. Of these, none appear to have been tried or executed. Several of them were pardoned upon application of their friends and others – and the rest, about 160 in number, were sent to Spain. Of the final disposition made of these we have no official information.

Such is the melancholy result of this illegal and ill-fated expedition. Thus, thoughtless young men have been induced, by false and fraudulent representations, to violate the law of their country through rash and unfounded expectations of assisting to accomplish political revolutions in other states and have lost their lives in the undertaking. Too severe a judgment can hardly be passed by the indignant sense of the community upon those who, being better informed themselves, have yet led away the ardor of youth and an ill-directed love of political liberty. The correspondence between this Government and that of Spain relating to this transaction is herewith communicated.

But what gives a peculiar criminality to this invasion of Cuba is that, under the lead of Spanish subjects and with the aid of citizens of the United States, it had its origin with many in motives of cupidity. Money was advanced by individuals, probably in considerable amounts, to purchase Cuban bonds, as they have been called, issued by López, sold, doubtless, at a very large discount, and for the payment of which the public lands and public property of Cuba, of whatever kind, and the fiscal resources of the people and government of that island, from whatever source to be derived, were pledged, as well as the good faith of the government expected to be established. All these means of payment, it is evident, were only to be obtained by a process of bloodshed, war and revolution. None will deny that those who set, on foot, military expeditions against foreign states by means like these, are far more culpable than the ignorant and the necessitous whom they induced to go forth as the ostensible parties in the proceeding. These originators of the invasion of Cuba seem to have determined, with coolness and system, upon an undertaking which should disgrace their country, violate its laws, and put to hazard the lives of ill-informed and deluded men. You will consider whether further legislation be necessary to prevent the perpetration of such offenses in future.

The occurrence at New Orleans has led me to give my attention to the state of our laws regarding foreign ambassadors, ministers and consuls. I think the legislation of the country is deficient in not providing sufficiently, either for the protection or the punishment of consuls. I therefore recommend the subject to the consideration of the congress."

CHAPTER17
CLEMENCY-THE JOURNEY HOME

Queen Isabella II took much consideration in President Fillmore's plea for the Cuban prisoners through D.M. Barringer, Minister of State in Madrid. Mr. Barringer went to the palace and spoke with his Excellency the Marquis of Miraflores. Through communications with Queen Isabella, she granted clemency for the prisoners of the López Expedition. She spoke in the highest terms, with respect for the American Government. The men were finally pardoned on December 10th by Queen Isabella of Spain.

In lieu of the Spanish riots that occurred in New Orleans on August 21st, the Spanish Consulate and twenty-two private individuals, in New Orleans and Key West, were given $83,813.70 by the American Government.

This was to help rebuild and restore the Spanish community with their businesses and to compensate private individuals. Naturally, no revenge was taken by the United States government for the murder of the soldiers and filibusters as they had voluntarily put themselves beyond the Neutrality Act.

The filibusters received the news of their release on

December 15th. As there was no American Consul in Vigo, the English Consul gave the men clothes and set up residence until the ship arrived for their departure back to the United States.

While the men waited for the ship, they discovered, before they left Havana, the American and English residents of that city had made a collection for the prisoners. The residents collected fifteen hundred dollars, to be turned over to Captain Ortiz of the *Guatemala*. This money was to be divided amongst the prisoners when they reached Spain. William said, "We received $5 dollars of this hoard. If you paid over a dime for anything, you were liable to get about a hatful of coppers in change." Having five dollars amounted to untold wealth in Vigo.

President Fillmore sent a letter to U.S. Senate and House of Representatives, stating the following:

"Be it enacted by the Senate and House of Representatives of the United States in Congress assembled. That there be, and hereby is appropriated, the sum of six thousand dollars or so much thereof as may be necessary, out of any money in the Treasury not otherwise appropriated, for the relief of American citizens lately imprisoned and pardoned by the Queen of Spain and who are out of the limits of the United States; the same to be expended under the direction of the President of the United States: Provided, that nothing in this act shall be construed into an approbation of any interference in the domestic affairs of Cuba by any of the citizens of the United States."

Approved February 10, 1852

Over the next several days, thirty or forty of the men were under English protection and were sent back to their homes in England. Thirty of the German prisoners were held for further orders.

William said his goodbyes to the men he fought so bravely with in Cuba. He waited a few more weeks until a passage could be obtained to the United States with the remaining men.

President Fillmore worked diligently to get the prisoners home. He provided forty dollars a person for ninety-five of the prisoners to return safely to the United States. Their daily necessities where taken care of and the men were now looking forward to going home.

An American vessel arrived seven weeks later in Vigo for the men. The voyage across the Atlantic Ocean would take them approximately a month. The ship, *Prentice*, Commander Woodbury, arrived in New York City on Saturday morning on March 13, 1852. Ninety-five men were welcomed as heroes, even though they were defeated. The news of their arrival quickly spread throughout the city. The people were wanting to see the men who had gone with López on the expedition to Cuba and escaped the grasp of Spain. The wharves filled with people, as they cheered when the ship finally docked.

They were entertained free of charge at three of the largest hotels in the city. One of the hotels was the North American Hotel. In honor of the fallen men on the expedition, the men wore a blue ribbon which distinguished them as one of the López Expedition survivors. William was on American soil and able to sleep in a comfortable bed again. Benefits were given at local theaters to raise money to help the survivors go back to their families. One of the benefits given was the 'Madame Sherwood's Benefit.' They were the distinguished American equestrian performers of all the most celebrated equestrian establishments in America. The prisoners were invited and appeared at the Bowery Amphitheater on Thursday, March 18th.

The men who joined López's Expedition and suffered so dearly, were able to separate in many directions and return to their families. They said their goodbyes to each other, after being together for such a long time and through the worst event anyone could endure. The men received enough money to reach their homes through the benefits that were given for them. Through their whole ordeal in Spain, the prisoners said they were treated fairly and had no complaints of the treatment from Spanish authorities.

William and thirty-four other men, who survived the López Expedition, set sail from New York, on the ship *Southerner*, on March 26th, to New Orleans. The ship *Southerner* was a mail courier at the time and made frequent stops before reaching New Orleans. When they finally reached New Orleans on April 15th, they were welcomed by friends and families. People from all over the south heard of them coming home and filled the streets while they waited with anticipation along the Mississippi River. Cannons were fired as a salute in honor of the filibusters upon their arrival.

CHAPTER 18
NEW ORLEANS CELEBRATES

The memory of General Narciso López was honored in New Orleans on September 1st, the anniversary of his death. The day started with the rapid, simultaneous discharge of fifty guns as the sounds of the artillery blasted through the air. Throughout the city, the people could hear the deep sounds echoing through the streets. The St. Louis Cathedral's great organ bellowed throughout the square as everyone turned and listened to every note being played. The bells of the tower mingled with the choir in a synchronized symphony. Crowds gathered in the streets of the French Quarter, with their heads bowed, in a state of sorrow for the fallen men who lost their lives. Large crowds gathered at the cathedral's doors to peek inside.

Ceremonies began promptly at seven thirty in the morning. The pews were filled and the aisles were standing room only so the visitors could give their sympathies and respect for the memories of the dead. The choir's voice was like the sound of angels as the congregation remained silent over the next two hours. A final prayer was said, with every head bowed, and the service was over. The people slowly headed for the large wooden doors at the front entrance. They were all united in the love of liberty and in their admiration and appreciation of those who had suffered for such a tragic cause.

The *Pampero* was docked at one of the wharves nearby to commemorate the solemn occasion for the filibusters. She had flown the flag of the expedition at half-mast. Throughout the day, people thought about López, Crittenden, Kerr and all the other men who lost their lives. A torchlight procession gathered in the streets at seven thirty that evening, in front of the St. Louis Cathedral on Chartres Street. After thousands had assembled for the procession, they started towards St. Ann Street. They turned left on St. Ann Street and continued until they reached Royal Street. The entire population of the city appeared to be out, crowding the streets throughout where the procession was to pass. Cheers could be heard from the balconies above the cobblestone streets as they walked and raised their fire-lit torches. The procession itself was one of the largest that ever turned out at night in the city of New Orleans. It was a combination of citizens from all nationalities and professions, even though the people may have felt differently regarding religious and political beliefs.

The procession continued and turned left on Royal Street. The cheers continued as they passed by many businesses and homes along the way. At the head of the procession was the Grand Marshall, Colonel C. R. Wheat, accompanied by his aids. Then came the military escort, compiled of a Washington Regiment under Colonel W.

Wood. Next, the hearse, driven by four white horses, was accompanied by a number of Creoles of Cuba as pall bearers. General López's noble officer's Colonel William Scott Haynes and Major Kelly followed closely behind. William and the men who lived in New Orleans who had fought so bravely as soldiers of liberty with the López Expedition, carried a banner. Inscribed on the banner were the words: "The Returned Cuban Prisoners – beaten, but not conquered!"

They continued on Royal Street till they crossed Canal Street which turns into St. Charles Avenue. The torches the men were carrying lit up the entire street as the light glimmered through the trees. More people were now following the procession. After the men carrying the banner, came the patriotic and generous Firemen of New Orleans. The rear of the procession was a long line of horse drawn carriages with a large representation of Cuban Creoles who had a deep awareness of the occasion. In between the divisions of the honored men, throughout the procession, were the musicians of the city, who played during the entire route. Continuing down St. Charles Avenue, they headed towards Julia Street. People continued to cheer and crowded the streets along the way to get a glimpse of the survivors of the López Expedition. They turned left on Julia Street till they reached the end of the block at Camp Street. The procession turned left on Camp Street and now headed straight for Lafayette Square, where a huge crowd waited for them to arrive.

New Orleans had never seen such a display, which

excited a more unanimous and harmonious feeling, that occurred on that day. After the procession entered Lafayette Square, the large crowds of people formed around the stand. The speeches from men that were given, commenced with applause and cheers. The entire procession was 1.4 miles.

CHAPTER 19
CIVIL WAR WITH BENJAMIN BUTLER

William had gone through many dangers and suffering from the López Expedition. Still, he had the desire to see more. He decided to take an offer given to him and go to Central America to the island of Roatán. This island is located about forty miles off the northern coast of Honduras in the Caribbean Sea. After arriving at Roatán, he took charge of two banana plantations. Small shipments of bananas from the Bay Islands to the city of New Orleans was a big industry for the city's port. American and British citizens' demand for the fruit was insatiable. The export of fresh fruit, particularly bananas, plantains and coconuts, developed into a big business in Roatán.

William enjoyed the tropical climate and thought this was for him. While he was in charge of the plantations for a number of years, the Chagres fever was encountered on the island. William was in fear for his health and returned to New Orleans.

On his arrival in New Orleans he "narrowly missed being a member of the Walker expedition." His skills working with medicines began a new career as a druggist. William was stationed at the Pensacola Navy

Yard during the war till the "Federals blew it about their ears" William said. Most Southern troops were transferred out of Florida and William was one of them. By 1862, Confederate forces completely withdrew from Pensacola.

After being transferred to New Orleans, he positioned himself on the Steamer *Star of the West* as a druggist. *Star of the West* was a naval station and hospital ship until Admiral David Farragut captured New Orleans on April 29, 1862. Still under Confederate control, the *Star of the West* escaped the recapture by transporting the contents to Vicksburg and continuing to Yazoo City, Mississippi. When Major General Benjamin Butler took New Orleans, it was this steamer that escaped up the Mississippi River with gold and silver from the New Orleans Mint. William had no idea these valuables were on board and continued to administer help to the men, when he could, during the voyage up the Mississippi River. William was discharged at Jackson, Mississippi, and headed back to New Orleans once again – but he was captured by the Federals and taken before Butler.

"Would you like to go to Ship Island?" asked Butler suavely.

Ship Island was a desolate barrier island, twelve miles off the coast of Mississippi in the Gulf of Mexico, with a Union stronghold led by Butler. "Of course, no one wanted to go to Ship Island and this man expressed a deep-rooted aversion; the other alternative was to go in the Barrack's hospital and go to work."

New Orleans Barracks was allocated as a post for sending and receiving troops and became the first Public Service Hospital for Veterans in the United States. In 1861, Louisiana seceded from the United States and the Barracks was in the hands of Confederate forces for less than a year. The Union forces recaptured the Barracks and took control of the facilities in 1862. William went to work for eight months at the New Orleans Barracks, virtually the only druggist in the hospital. From fifteen hundred to eighteen hundred cases were treated daily.

Benjamin Butler served as a Major General in the Union Army and became a despised figure in the South during the Union occupation of New Orleans. He took military charge over the city on May 1, 1862 with five thousand Union soldiers. Once in New Orleans, he commanded the city, in rather controversial ways, as the appointed Military Governor. He was infamous in New Orleans for his confrontational proclamations and corruption, while the citizens called him disgraceful. Although he was able to bring order to the city, he became known as one who would take goods from the Southern households he was overlooking. He was considered hostile, but used his personal money to purchase food for the people who were poor and needy.

Confederate President Jefferson Davis labeled Butler as an outlaw and earned him the nickname ' Beast Butler' by Southern whites. One of Butler's quotes was noted for saying, "I was always a friend of Southern rights but an enemy of Southern wrongs." New Orleans was the apex of his military career. He commanded New Orleans with harsh rules and regulations but left the city in far better shape than in which he found it.

CHAPTER 20
MR. COUSANS
FINDS PEACE

Mr. Cousans secured employment with Haan & Frederickson's drugstore, for fifteen years, in the Touro buildings located on Canal Street in New Orleans. He married Julia Brady on May 21, 1862 at St. Joseph's Church on Tulane Avenue in New Orleans. Julia came from Sligo, Ireland, born in 1836 and came to New Orleans when she was just fifteen with her mother. William and Julia decided they had enough of the big city life in New Orleans and decided to move to Biloxi, Mississippi. They wanted to be near the water and the beach with their children and live a more peaceful life. William and Julia had seven children in their marriage. They remained together for over fifty years. The names of their children were Charles, Louisa, Alice, Susan, William, Thomas and Julia.

In Biloxi, William secured employment in the J.W. Swetman Drug Store as a prescription clerk. He remained there for more than twenty-five years, helping people in the community with ailments and whatever else was needed. He made many friends along the way and knew most of his customers on a first name basis. He stayed with the Swetman Drug Store until his retirement. This did not keep William from being active, for he loved the soil. He kept a garden, which he cultivated next to his home, and grew many vegetables and few flowers. He cared for it as long as he could until he was physically no longer able to care for it any longer.

William was a man of ideal character with all the love and tenderness of a husband, father and a friend to many. A man with the influence which held the closest of friends he made, wherever he went. His war record was one of proud distinction. Besides his war record, William had done much to aid the suffering in his community. Many ailments were treated by his prescriptions when a doctor was not to be found. His kind words and caring advice helped many people who would come to see him.

Mr. William Cousans passed away quietly at eleven twenty on the evening of June 29, 1925, at the age of ninety-two, in his home in Biloxi. His family stayed close to his side. His wife, Julia, was not with him, having died several years before. His funeral was accompanied by three Confederate veterans from the Jefferson Davis Soldiers Home in Biloxi, who represented three comrades who served with him during the Civil War. He was laid to rest with full military honors and closed with Taps playing in the background. He was survived by three daughters and two sons. The large family also consisted of twenty-three grandchildren and fifteen great grandchildren, who were also present for his funeral.

He survived through perseverance and honor

throughout the López Expedition, Civil War and afterwards. He never gave up and continued to go on. Because of his will and determination, many generations have come to life because of William.

CHAPTER 21
IN HONOR OF THE FILIBUSTERS...

Prisoners aboard the *Primera de Guatemala* sent to Spain:

Name	Age	State/Country	Trade
Albing, James	21	New York	Boatman
Alfonso, Antonio L.	31	Havana	Doctor
Alleno, Bernard	18	Ireland	Carpenter
Arman, Ramon Ignacio	31	Cuba	Penman
Badneih, Emerich	27	Hungary	Soldier
Baltar, James D.	25	Indiana	Clerk
Bauder, Louis	37	Germany	Barkeeper
Bell, Edwin Q.	20	South Carolina	Clerk
Biro, Michael	26	Poland	Soldier
Bontila, George	26	Hungary	Merchant
Boswel, John	25	Maryland	Mason
Bournazal, Pierre Charles de	40	France	Tailor
Boyd, Franklin P.	21	New York	Engineer
Brady, James	26	Isle of Wright	Laborer
Bush, John G.	24	Virginia	Printer

Cajerman, James	19	South Carolina	Carpenter
Cameron, William H.	45	Virginia	Carpenter
Carts, John	26	Illinois	Carpenter
Casanova, JoaQuin	32	Louisiana	Clerk
Chassagne, Julio	27	Cuba	Silversmith
Ciceri, Joseph	19	Hungary	Soldier
Cichler, Conrad	23	Hungary	Printer
Coleman, Patrick	29	Ireland	Laborer
Constantine, W.B.	21	Canada	Painter
Cook, Cornelius	21	Alabama	Printer
Cooper, John	19	Virginia	Clerk
Cousans, William	19	England	Clerk
Craft, William H.	23	Virginia	Courier
Crissy, Edgard	27	Pennsylvania	Painter
Cully, Supe L.	20	Ireland	Carpenter
Daily, Thomas	19	Ireland	Clerk
Denton, John	28	New York	Clerk
Denton, Thomas	22	New York	Carpenter
Diaz, Manuel	34	Cuba	Merchant
Dupart, Victor	19	Louisiana	Engineer

Fagin, James Benjamin	19	Ohio	Boatman
Fontz, Jacob	20	Germany	Butcher
Fleuri, Manuel	22	Cuba	Printer
Garth, Patrick Abac	28	Ireland	Laborer
Geblin, Charles	23	Pennsylvania	Boatman
Gilmore, Benjamin	19	Ohio	Bricklayer
Grider, Robert H.	34	Kentucky	Merchant
Guerro, Miguel	28	Cuba	Shoemaker
Gunst, Joseph B.	16	Louisiana	Clerk
Hagan, Lewis	22	Germany	Confectioner
Hanna, Benjamin F.	29	Pennsylvania	Farmer
Harrison, Charles	21	Louisiana	Painter
Hart, Henry B.	22	Pennsylvania	Engineer
Hearsey, James H.	25	Louisiana	Clerk
Hefron, Michael L.	21	New York	Steward
Henry, Timothy K.	32	Ireland	Clerk
Hernandez, Antonio	22	Cuba	Painter
Hider, Thomas	26	Washington, D.C.	Painter
Holdship, George	20	Pennsylvania	Boatman
Horwell, Charles	23	Virginia	Printer

Hudnall, Thomas	35	Virginia	Farmer
Hurd, William K.	16	Louisiana	Clerk
Iglesias, Francisco	24	Cuba	Laborer
Iwin, James G.	21	England	Merchant
Joster, George W.	17	New York	Laborer
Kercker, Bela	22	Hungary	Soldier
Lacoste, Peter	21	Louisiana	Driver
Laine, Francisco Alejandro	27	Cuba	Overseer
Lee, Thomas H.	19	England	Clerk
Lopez, Pedro Manuel	24	Venezuela	Merchant
Ludwing, Ansell R.	28	Maine	Seaman
Mahan, Francis C.	23	Kentucky	Farmer
Martinez, Manuel	35	Cuba	Tobacconist
McLeabe, Bernard	23	Ireland	Laborer
McClelland, Thomas	22	Ireland	Shoemaker
McKensey, William H.	18	Kentucky	Bricklayer
McKneiss, John	26	Pennsylvania	Boatman
McMullen, Peter D.	20	Maine	Cook
McMurray, C.A.	21	Maryland	Printer
Melesimo, Martin	29	Cuba	Tobacconist

Melcalf, George E.	22	Ohio	Druggist
Melcalf, Henry B.	19	Mississippi	Druggist
Monroe, Thomas R.	20	Alabama	Machinist
Meallen, Martin	19	Ireland	Cook
Murphy, John	23	Ireland	Waiter
Nelson, Richard	39	Denmark	Unknown
Ninkos, Janos	23	Hungary	Soldier
Nolasco, Pedro	18	Cuba	Cook
Null, Charles	24	Germany	Baker
Olis, Elijah J.	22	New York	Boatman
Paratolt, Conrad	17	Germany	Clerk
Petrie, John	23	Hungary	Soldier
Pruitt, John R.	24	Alabama	Printer
Purnell, Stephen Howard	20	Mississippi	Printer
Romero, Antonio	26	Cuba	Laborer
Rousseau, David Q.	24	Kentucky	Bricklayer
Sarmeron, Eduardo	27	Cuba	Shoemaker
Sayle, Henry	29	England	Molder
Schluht, Harbo	29	Germany	Soldier
Schmidt, George	21	Germany	Laborer

Schmidt, Henry	21	Germany	Butcher
Schuetz, Robert	24	Germany	Joiner
Scott, Malbon K.	20	Kentucky	Courier
Seay, Dandridge (Daniel)	21	South Carolina	Engineer
Sebring, Cornelius	25	New York	Laborer
Scheiprt, Zyriack	34	Germany	Watchmaker
Simpson, J.P.	23	Pennsylvania	Butcher
Smith, James	29	Massachusetts	Farmer
Stanmire, Henry	26	Pennsylvania	Unknown
Taylor, Conrad	24	Germany	Cook
Vaughn, William H.	40	Kentucky	Clerk
Virag, Janos	24	Hungary	Soldier
Weiss, Edward	22	Germany	Butcher
West, Henry	26	Ohio	Saddler
Williams, Harvey	48	Connecticut	Farmer
Wilson, George R.	21	Pennsylvania	Japanner
Wilson, James M.	22	Indiana	Clerk
Wilson, William	22	New York	Clerk
Wilson, William	18	Kentucky	Boatman
Wilkinson, William L.	25	Alabama	Engineer

Winburn, David	37	South Carolina	Bricklayer

Prisoners aboard the *Isabel la Catolica* sent to Spain:

Downer, Charles A.	23	Alabama	Clerk
Hughes, Joel D.	--	Louisiana	Unknown
Hough, Fenton D.	19	Indiana	Engineer

Prisoners aboard the *Venus* sent to Spain:

Schlessinger, Louis	--	Hungry	Soldier
McDonald, Edmund	20	Alabama	Clerk
Norriss, John	--	Alabama	Unknown
DeWolf, Daniel E.	23	Alabama	Clerk
Thomason, H.J.	18	Alabama	Clerk
Wier, Armand R.	22	Alabama	Clerk

Prisoners aboard the ship *Ripa* to Spain:

Batchelder, John	40	Massachusetts	Carpenter
Beach, Ransom	26	Kentucky	Butcher
Berry, George S.	23	Ohio	Carpenter

Breckenridge, H.	35	Kentucky	Laborer
Brown, John	25	Ohio	Carpenter
Brown, Thomas D.	25	Louisiana	Driver
Bryam, Thomas	25	Kentucky	Farmer
Cay, Eugene N.	20	England	Engineer
Clyne, John	21	Pennsylvania	Boatman
Conelly, Edward	24	Ireland	Painter
David, John N.	35	England	Blacksmith
Doran, Jose	45	Cuba	Laborer
Doyle, John	20	England	Laborer
Duffy, Cornelius G.	17	Massachusetts	Clerk
Essex, Preston	25	Ireland	Carpenter
Freeborn, Isaac	38	Ohio	Tailor
Garcia, Feo. Curbia	39	Cuba	Merchant
Geiger, Michael	23	France	Driver
Gonzales, Andrew	21	New Granada	Machinist
Haguin, Alexander	36	Germany	Clerk
Harrison, George	37	Columbia	Carpenter
Johnson, John	35	Kentucky	Merchant
Little, Thomas	30	Pennsylvania	Carpenter

Losner, William	22	Germany	Boatman
Lyons, Michael	26	Ireland	Laborer
McNeil, Thomas L.	23	South Carolina	Clerk
Miller, William	32	Louisiana	Shoemaker
Montevo, Aug.	35	Cuba	Merchant
Myers, James	22	Ireland	Merchant
Myers, Joseph	24	Ireland	Merchant
Nagle, Louis	28	Missouri	Unknown
Parr, George	25	Louisiana	Painter
Philips, Asher T.	21	Louisiana	Painter
Port, Nicholas	19	France	Clerk
Porter, Thomas T.	23	Ireland	Clerk
Robinson, John	20	England	Boatman
Seifort, John	28	Indiana	Carpenter
Smith, John F.	24	Ireland	Machinist
Sowers, J. Albert	20	England	Laborer
Stevens, Joseph	26	New York	Carpenter
Talbot, John	19	Ireland	Clerk
Waymouth, Joseph	48	New Hampshire	Pilot
Young, William	25	Ireland	Butcher

Prisoners recovering in the hospital in Havana:

Name	Age	State/Country	Injury
Aragon, Manuel	--	Cuba	Arm
Col. Blummenthal	--	Washington D.C.	--
Curvia, F.	--	Cuba	Arm
Douvren, Jose	--	Cuba	Side
Edgerton, George	--	Mississippi	Sick
Ellis, Robert H.	22	Washington D.C.	Left Hand
Fiddes, James	--	Malta	Both legs
Gano, David	--	New York	--
Hodge, Charles J.	--	England	--
Jasper, Henry	--	Germany	Foot
Jessert, Jacob	--	Unknown	--
Keenan, M.J.	--	Alabama	Finger
Miller, William	32	England	Finger
Palanka, L.	--	Hungary	--
Porter, J.G.	--	Ireland	Chest/Arm
Richardson, George	--	Louisiana	Arm
Rieves, Wilson L.	--	Mississippi	--
Rubria, J.B.	--	Spain	--
Talbot, John	--	Louisiana	Hand

Before the prisoners boarded for their sentence to Spain, they addressed a letter to Mr. Smith, the Secretary of the British Consul:

Castle of La Punta, Havana, Saturday, September 27, 1851.

"Gentlemen: We the undersigned, prisoners now confined in the Castillo la Punta, on the eve of our departure for Spain cannot refrain from expressing our most heartfelt gratitude for the unwearied exertions you have used in our behalf, and the repeated acts of kindness which have tendered so much to alleviate the sufferings, which we have nearly forgotten; your generosity having left us nothing to wish for but liberty.

With our best wishes for your health, happiness and prosperity, we bid you adieu, with the hope that the day is not far distant when we shall have the pleasure of welcoming you the United States.

We are, very respectfully, your friends.

Signed by 45 names"

Prisoners pardoned from the Captain General Concha of Cuba:

Lieutenant Chapman, James	-	South Carolina	Officer
Colonel Haynes, Scott	-	Louisiana	Officer
Captain Kelly, J.A.	-	Louisiana	Officer

Lieutenant, Somers, H.G.	-	Louisiana	Officer
Lieutenant Van Vechten, P.S.	-	New York	Officer

The men executed on August 16, 1851, Havana:

Officers:

Colonel Crittenden, William Logan

Captain Kerr, Victor

Captain Sawyer, Fred S.

Captain Vesey, T.S.

Lieutenant Brandt, James

Lieutenant Bryce, John O.

Lieutenant James, Thomas C.

Adjutant Stanford, R.C. Surgeon

Forniquet, H. Surgeon

Fisher, John Sergeant Collins,

Napoleon Sergeant Crockett,

A.M. Sergeant Green, G.M.

Sergeant Salmon, J.M.

Sergeant Witherens, J.A.

Soldiers:

Arnold, George W.

Ball, M.H.

Burrourk, P.

Bylet, James

Caldwell, Robert

Cantley, Robert

Chilling, William

Christides, John

Collins, E.T.
Cook, Gilman A.
Dillon, Patrick
Ellis, James
Fisher, N.H.
Hartnett, Thomas
Hearsey, Thomas
Hernandez, Anselmo Torres
Hogan, William
Holmes, William H.
Jones, S.C.
Little, William B.
McIlcer, Alexander
Manville, James L.
Mills, Samuel
Niceman, William
Phillips, M.
Reed, Samuel
Robinson, Charles A.
Ross, A.
Rulman, Edward
Sanka, John G.
Smith, C.C. William
Stanton, James
Stubbs, John J.
Vienne, H. T.
Wregy, B. J.

Many of the filibusters were killed in battle or never seen again. They joined the expedition to free Cuba from the oppression of Spain, paying the ultimate price.

These unknown men carried onward with the horrors they had to endure. From mountain highs to valley lows, they gave their life in the honor of freedom. We cannot forget their honor, bravery and the sacrifices they gave for this expedition, never to return home.

Had the Creoles risen, as they were expected, this little handful of brave men might have been the means of establishing Cuban independence. The memory of their valor will be remembered throughout generations to come. Fifty-one years after the last López Expedition, Cuba obtained their independence, so that we can afford to believe that the blood of all the men who died and suffered was not shed in vain.

References:

- *The Times Democrat*, Louisiana, March 30, 1913
- *The Weekly Iberian*, Louisiana, February 15, 1913
- Find a Grave
- Wikipedia
- *Brief History of the French Quarter*, By: Sally Reeves
- *The Register of the Kentucky Historical Society*, By: Colonel M.C. Taylor's Diary
- History of Venezuela
- *Lopez's Expeditions to Cuba, 1850 and 1851*, By: Anderson Chenault Quisenberry
- Journal of the Early Republic
- Biography
- University of North Texas, *The Expeditions of Narciso Lopez and the South, 1850-1851*
- *Slavocracy and Empire, New Orleans and the Attempted Expansion of Slavery, 1845-1861*, By: C. Stanley Urban
- *Cuban Filibustering in Jacksonville in 1851*, By: Antonio Rafael de la Cova
- *The Times Democrat*, Louisiana, April 6, 1884
- *The Journal of the Jacksonville Historical Society*, 1996
- Forgotten Books – *Lopez's Expeditions to Cuba 1850 and 1851*

- Encyclopedia Virginia
- Almost Chosen People
- History
- *The Lopez Expeditions to Cuba 1848-1851*, By: Robert Granville Caldwell
- The Crittenden Memoirs, By: Philip Kromer
- *The Free Flag of Cuba*: The Lost Novel of Lucy Holcombe Pickens
- The Legend of the St. James Hotel, New Orleans
- Manifest Destiny's Underworld: *Filibustering in Antebellum American*, By: Robert E. May
- Dictionary
- *Last in Their Class, Custer, Pickett and the Goats of West Point*, By: James S. Robbins
- Personal Narrative of Louis Schlesinger of, *Adventures in Cuba and Ceuta*
- *Cuba in 1851, Authentic Statistics of the Population, Agriculture and Commerce of the Island for a series of years, with official and other documents*, By: Alexander Jones
- *History of New Orleans*, By John Kendall
- *Life of General Lopez and History of the Late Attempted Revolution in Cuba*, By: A Filbustiero
- Castles and Other Fortifications in Europe and Beyond!
- *The Daily Picayune*, Louisiana, August 22, 1851
- Edinburgh and London Edition of Chamber's Encyclopedia
- *Cuba 1851, A Survey of the Island*, By: Alexander Jones
- *Gallipolis Journal*, Ohio, August 28, 1851

- *The Republic Volume*, Washington D.C., August 25, 1851
- *Wheeling Daily Intelligencer*, West Virginia, December 3, 1852
- *The Gulf States Historical Magazine*, Alabama, July, 1903
- Executed today, Colonel William Logan Crittenden
- *The History of Cuba*, By: Willis Fletcher Johnson
- *The Relations of the United States and Spain Diplomacy*, By: French Ensor Chadwick
- United States National Archives, General Records of the State Department, Miscellaneous Correspondence 1784-1906
- *The American Consul, A History of the United States Consular Service, 1776-1924*, By: Charles Stuart Kennedy
- *The Portsmouth Inquirer*, Ohio, October 31, 1851
- *The Primitive Republican*, Mississippi, October 7, 1851
- *Appendix to the Congressional Globe, Assaults on the Spanish Consul, Senate and House of Representatives*, By: E.A. Bradford
- *Gallipolis Journal*, Ohio, September 11, 1851
- *A Digest of International Law*, By: Alexander Jones
- *The St. Louis and the St. Charles New Orleans Legacy of Showcase Exchange Hotels*, By: Richard Campanella
- Weekly National Intelligencer, Washington D.C., September 6, 1851

- *Gentle Tiger, The Gallant Life of Roberdeau Wheat,* By: Charles L. Dufour
- Lafayette Square Conservancy
- *Index To The Executive Documents, Thirty Second Congress,* By: Mayor Mayoralty of New Orleans, August 21, 1851
- *Hoosier State Chronicles,* Indiana, September 4, 1851
- *Richmond Enquirer,* Virginia, August 26, 1851
- *Fortified Coast Towns of Cuba,* Michigan, November 21, 1873
- *Indiana State Sentinel,* Indiana, September 18, 1851
- Famous Wonders
- *The New York Herald,* New York, September 13, 1851
- *The North Carolinian Volume,* North Carolina, October 4, 1851
- *Hand Book of Universal Geography being a Gazetteer of the World,* By: T. Carey Callicot
- American History from Revolution to Reconstruction and Beyond, December 2, 1851
- Index to the Executive Documents, Thirty Second Congress, January 6, 1852
- The Executive Documents of the House of Representatives for the Second Session of the Forty Ninth Congress Foreign Relations
- *Northern Democrat,* New York, March 18, 1852
- The Statutes at Large and Treaties of the United States of America, December 1, 1851 to March 3, 1855, Millard Fillmore

- *The Congressional Globe: The Debates, Proceedings, and Laws, of the First Session of the Thirty Second Congress*, By: John C. Rives, W. Hunter
- *The Southern Press*, Washington D.C., March 22, 1852
- *New York Daily Tribune*, New York, March 18, 1852
- *Baton Rouge Gazette*, Louisiana, April 17, 1852
- *New Orleans Daily Crescent*, Louisiana, April 16, 1852
- *The Mountain Sentinel*, Pennsylvania, September 23, 1852
- New Orleans Official Guide
- *Star of the West*
- Ship Island Excursions, 1926
- Saving America's Civil War Battlefields
- Family Papers
- *New Orleans Republican*, Louisiana, June 7, 1874
- Encyclopedia Britannica

Made in the USA
Columbia, SC
20 May 2018